Flee My Father's House

Flee My Father's House

Kay Rizzo

*Knowing she can
never love the man
her father commands
her to marry, Chloe
makes her choice.
But will she ever
find her dream?*

Pacific Press Publishing Association
Boise, Idaho
Oshawa, Ontario, Canada

Edited by Bonnie Widicker
Designed by Tim Larson
Cover photograph by Sinclair Studios
Typeset in 11/13 New Century Schoolbook

Copyright © 1993 by
Pacific Press Publishing Association
Printed in the United States of America
All Rights Reserved

Library of Congress Cataloging-in-Publication Data:

Rizzo, Kay D., 1943-
    Flee my father's house / Kay D. Rizzo.
        p.   cm.
    ISBN 0-8163-1134-X   paper
    ISBN 0-8163-1154-4   hardcover
    I. Title.
PS3568. I836F57 1993
813'.54—dc20   92-33707
                                                    CIP

93 94 95 96 97 ● 5 4 3 2 1

Dedication

To Mom Rizzo . . .
a pioneer in the finest sense

Acknowledgments

Richard Rizzo, for being my secretary, my personal editor, my slave driver, and for being the cutest cheerleader on my squad.

Marvin Moore, for his faith in the project and in me.

Gene and Sue Haynes, for their knowledge of railroading.

Dr. Harry Cargenian of Goble/Miller Funeral Home, Tulare, California, for information on death certificates and burial permits.

Esta Lou Riley, curator for Special Collections, Western Kansas Archives, Fort Hays University, Hays, Kansas.

Dr. Gregory Quakenbush, D.V.M., Foothill Veterinary Clinic, Porterville, California.

Donald Snoddy, director of the Union Pacific Historical Museum, Omaha, Nebraska, for turn-of-the-century train schedules and trivia.

Bruce Hurd, public relations officer, AMTRAK, for his enthusiasm and helpfulness.

Bill Busch, of John Busch Modoc Mineral Exploration, Gridley, California, for his information on mines and mining in the early American West.

Contents

Growing Pains

Tears stung my eyes as rain drummed against my bedroom window. Angry clouds belched thunder, rattling the window panes. Frightened yet fascinated, I pressed my nose against the glass to better view my cozy little world going berserk.

A boom of thunder and a charge of lightning merged into one terrifying jolt. The sound of splintering followed by a crash tingled me with fear as a massive limb from the oak tree across the road hit the ground. *Poor Patches,* I thought, *he's probably cowering under the front porch.*

I glanced about the eerie black-and-gray world inside my bedroom. Even the red-and-yellow calico quilt draped about my shoulders looked gray. I buried my face in my arms. The violence of the lightning storm mirrored the hurricane growing within me. My tumbling thoughts pushed and shoved like a batch of kids yammering for licorice sticks.

Growing up isn't fair! If I had my way, I'd stay ten years old forever. That's the year before Worley, my pesky brother, was born and before my older sister, Hattie, broke her hip by falling off the back of the wagon during a church hayride. The six years since had grown nothing but worse. I hardly noticed when my oldest brother, Riley, left home to work as foreman for Mr. Holmes, a gentleman farmer, or when my second oldest brother, Joe, got a day job at the Chamberlain stables.

However, when Hattie's twin, Myrtle, married Franklin Stone and moved into town, my childhood came to an end. Overnight, I was expected to pick up Myrtle's share of the household and farm chores while my former responsibilities moved down the line to my little sister, Orinda, Ori for short.

I learned early that being the fifth child in a large family had its advantages. At times, my rank allowed me to become almost invisible. Whenever I found the work too disagreeable or the task too boring, I'd pass it down to a younger brother or sister. If that plan failed, I'd complain until, in sheer desperation, Ma would assign the chore to one of my older siblings. And if worst came to worst, I would wait until no one was watching, then sneak away to my own special hiding place, a room in the attic of the barn where Pa dried and stored his herbs.

The sight and smell of drying mustard, parsley, and oregano plants hanging from the rafters made me feel safe. I knew better than to touch any of the containers or tamper with the assortment of tools strewn across Pa's heavy oak workbench.

Tucked under the eaves, behind a massive camelback trunk where Ma kept her treasures from Ireland, I stored my treasures, a stack of books from the town library. There I would curl up with the family mongrel, Patches, and read by the light seeping in between the wallboards until either the daylight faded, the crisis passed, or the next mealtime arrived. Other times I would sit on the floor with my arms wrapped around my knees and watch my father create his healing elixirs.

Joseph Riley Spencer's knowledge of herbs came from his Scottish grandmother, Chloe Mae McRiley, after whom I was named. Since the only other medical person, Doc Simms, lived in the town of Bradford, on the western side of Potter County, Pa assumed the responsibility of caring for our neighbors as best he could. He depended on Auntie Gert, the local midwife, to take charge of the birthings.

In addition to his medical practice and the small herd of Jerseys he milked, Pa worked for the Standard Oil Company as a pipeline inspector. His job was to check the pipes for leaks and damage. Whenever I wasn't in school, he would take me with him.

On these excursions, Pa loved to talk politics, from the Indian uprisings out West to President Cleveland's money policy, from voting rights for women to Japan's war on China. He ranted against the railway strike in Chicago and praised the president for breaking it. He applauded the Woman's Christian Temperance Union's battle to destroy demon whiskey and cursed William Jennings Bryan for wanting to cheapen the nation's gold standard with silver. My father knew everything there was to know in the whole wide world. Whenever my enthusiasm bubbled over and I told him so, he would chuckle and tug one of my waist-length, flame-red braids.

"Chloe Mae, you're good for me," he would say. And I would tuck away the praise for the days I didn't feel quite so special. We shared something else—fiery red hair, freckles, and green eyes. The other children in the family inherited Ma's sandy brown hair. With the birth of each new baby, I secretly prayed that my specialness would remain intact.

The day my mother went into labor with Dorothy, my sister Hattie, Ma, and I spent the entire day in the backyard doing the family wash. Scrubbing canvas breeches and linsey-woolsey shirts was hard work. Good old Patches dodged between our feet, thinking the three of us were there for his pleasure. I had pinned the last sheet to the clothesline when I spotted Pa and my older brothers coming up the road.

I hurried around to the back of the house, where Ma and Hattie were dumping the rinse water. "Pa's comin' home."

Exhausted, Ma straightened and stroked her lower back. The bulge produced by the unborn baby threatened to topple her forward. "The men'll be wantin' supper right away, I suppose."

Hattie limped to Ma's side and guided her toward the house. "Now don't you worry about supper, Ma. Chloe and I can take care of everything."

I glared at Hattie. *Thank you very much for volunteering my services!* After all, I was tired too. My glare passed unheeded. Hattie wrapped an arm about Ma's shoulders and led her toward the back door. "Chloe, you finish up out here while I help Ma inside and get the johnnycake bakin'."

Grumbling about the unfairness of life, I dried out the washtubs and returned the laundry supplies to the storage shed. The aroma of bubbling hot vegetable stew erased all thoughts of mistreatment from my mind as I stepped inside the kitchen pantry. I could hear my seventeen-year-old brother, Joe, telling Hattie and the younger children about his first day of work at the Chamberlain stables.

Cyrus Chamberlain, Jr., the manager of Standard Oil Company's interests in Shinglehouse, as well as Pa's supervisor, owned the finest stables in Potter County. So when Mr. Chamberlain wanted to hire the finest groom in the county, neighbors recommended my brother Joe. Joe had a knack with horses. Pa said Joe spoke their language.

"How did it go today, Joe?" I called as I breezed into the kitchen through the pantry door. Amby, Jesse, and Worley sat at the table, eagerly listening to Joe, while my little sister Ori carried steaming bowls of stew to the table for Hattie.

"Oh, Chloe Mae, you should see those horses—every one of 'em a thoroughbred." For some reason, Joe and I always sought one another's approval. Now I was a bit jealous that he was being paid to do just what he wanted while I stayed at home, scrubbing dirty work pants on a washboard and chasing bratty little brothers and sisters out of the pantry.

"Humph!" I snorted. "Seems to me that a horse is a horse is a horse, regardless of its folks."

Pa stepped into the kitchen, closing my parents' bedroom door behind him. "Hardly! Bloodlines will tell in a quality horse or a quality human being. Look at all of you children—every one of you a thoroughbred."

We laughed as Pa sat down at the head of the table and opened the family Bible. "John 6:13: 'Therefore they gathered them together, and filled twelve baskets with the fragments of the five barley loaves, which remained over and above unto them that had eaten. Then those men . . .' "

As Pa read the story of Jesus feeding the five thousand, Amby's stomach growled in protest. Pa glanced his way and smiled. "Guess we have a few hungry stomachs of our own here tonight. What do you say we have the blessing?"

It didn't take long after Pa's amen to empty our bowls and to clean every crumb of corn bread from the platter in the center of the table. Hattie looked at our pitiful faces and laughed. "Don't worry; I made an extra pan of johnnycake."

While I dished up seconds of the stew, Hattie removed the second pan of corn bread from the oven. She turned to set the hot pan on the breadboard at the same moment I whirled about to place a bowl of stew in front of my nine-year-old brother, Jesse. Instinctively, I squealed and leapt back.

Hattie's limp prevented her from moving as quickly. The pan thumped to the floor as she lifted her hands to protect herself from the stew. The scalding liquid splashed across the palms of her hands and her bodice. She screamed in pain.

Pa leapt from the table and rushed her to the wet sink. Thrusting her hands under the spout of the pump, he grabbed the handle and began pumping. Well water gushed out onto her hands. "Hattie, keep your hands under the cool water. Joe, take over the pumping while I run to the barn for some burn ointment."

The younger children and I scrambled to clean up the food that spilled on the floor. Before Pa could return with the ointment, Patches started barking at the front door. Jesse looked out the hall window, then opened the door before the visitor could begin knocking. Pa entered the back door as George Neff, a farmer from over Sunnyside way, burst in through the front. "My son Merton fell off the roof of the barn. He's hurtin' real bad!"

"I'll get my doctorin' bag." Pa shoved the jar of ointment into Jesse's hand and ran into the bedroom. "Annie, will you be all right while I . . ."

I didn't hear my mother's reply, but within seconds, Pa reappeared. Grabbing his hunting jacket from the peg behind the door, he shouted orders at each of us. "Hattie, apply the ointment to your burns. Chloe, after you clean up here, get the little ones settled down for the night. Joe, you help her, especially with the boys." He shook his finger at six-year-old Worley. "And, you, young man, don't give Joe or Chloe a rough time, you hear?" Pa handed his medicine bag to Mr. Neff and hauled on his jacket.

"Chloe, keep checking on your mother. She's actin' like it's her time, but she has a good three weeks to go." Joe and I assured him we could take care of everything.

Joe put ointment on Hattie's burns while I heated a kettle of water on the stove for the supper dishes. He appointed twelve-year-old Amby to oversee the dishwashing crew before he helped Hattie upstairs to her room. When I finished cleaning the kitchen, I hurried upstairs. I found Hattie sitting on the edge of the bed, rocking back and forth and moaning.

"Oh, Hattie, I am so sorry. Honest, I didn't know you were right behind me." I wept as I guided the sleeves of her dress over her bandaged hands.

She smiled through her tears. "It was an accident. I should have looked where I was going."

By the time I tucked her in her bed, Ori appeared, her lower lip quivering with disappointment. "Joe says I'm supposed to go to bed, and without my story too!"

I scooped my little sister into my arms and carried her to the massive bed she and I shared. "If you hurry and get into your nightdress, I'll tell you a story while I brush out your braids, all right?"

The little girl nodded eagerly. She scurried about the room getting ready for bed. The sounds of my younger brothers' griping filled the stairwell as Joe herded them up to their room across the hall. *Thank goodness for Joe!* I thought. At least I didn't have to settle the boys down for the night.

When Ori finished dressing for bed, I unwound her braids and drew the hairbrush through her brown, shoulder-length mane. "Once upon a time there was a beautiful queen . . ." My imagination soared as I described my favorite Bible character. "Of course, Queen Esther had shimmering red hair."

"Oh, Chloe," Ori groaned. "The beautiful ladies in your stories always have to have red hair like yours."

"Because I'm the one telling the story. When you tell the story, you can make them have black hair or golden hair." I tickled her stomach. "Or no hair, for that matter!" She giggled. I guided my sister to the bed and tucked the covers up around her chin.

"Where was I? Oh, yes, the beautiful queen had long, fiery-red hair. That's what the handsome king fell in love with—her hair!" Ori snuggled down and closed her eyes. My story grew far beyond anything the Bible writers intended. Long before I executed the dastardly, evil Haman on his own gallows, my little sister was sound asleep. I brushed a stray curl from the sleeping child's face, kissed her forehead, then stood up. Tiptoeing to the side of Hattie's bed, I asked, "Are you going to be all right? Can I get you anything before I go downstairs to see about Ma?"

She shook her head. "I'll be fine."

I stole one last glimpse at the sleeping Ori and stepped out of the room. Joe met me in the hall. "Ma needs you. I think that baby isn't going to wait any three weeks to be born."

My eyes widened in horror. Pa was gone. Hattie couldn't deliver the baby with her burned hands. Myrtle was in town. So was Auntie Gert. Neither Joe nor I knew anything about birthing. I grabbed my skirt and petticoats and descended the stairs three at a time. Joe bounded after me, shushing my every step. "You're going to wake Worley!"

At that moment, I didn't particularly care as I rushed into my parents' bedroom. My mother lay on her side, moaning. Sweat beaded on her frighteningly pale face. Sweat drenched the pillowslip beneath her head. I pushed aside the locks of heavy brown hair pasted to her forehead.

Why would any woman in her right mind be willing go through such torture? I remembered Pa reading from Genesis about Eve's being cursed to bear children in pain. Right then and there, standing beside my parents' bed, I decided marriage and babies were absolutely not for me. And when I got to heaven, I'd have a thing or two to tell Mother Eve too.

Gathering my courage about me, I inched closer. Suddenly Ma's eyes flew open. She gasped, "Chloe, the baby's coming. Get Auntie Gert!"

"Oh, right—get Auntie Gert!" I bolted from the room, colliding with Joe in the doorway, his eyes bulging with fear.

"What are we going to do? Should I go for Pa?"

Terrified, I shouted in his face, "No, go get Auntie Gert!" As he ran to saddle Dulcie, a cry came from the bedroom. I whirled about and rushed back to my mother.

"Chloe! Forget Auntie Gert! The baby . . . just do as I . . ."

I leapt away from the cast-iron bedstead. "I can't! No! Joe's getting Auntie Gert."

My mother rolled her head from side to side and panted as if she'd run all the way to Haney's Mercantile without stopping. "No! I need you. Listen, do everything I say . . ." Her words crumbled into a grimace. When the contraction subsided, she moaned, "Get the birthing linens out of the chest at the foot of the bed. Go boil some water."

Step by step, she explained everything I would need to do throughout the delivery. Determined to carry out her instructions, I argued with myself all the way to the hand pump. *I can do this; I can do this! No, you can't; no, you can't!*

Standing in the middle of the kitchen, I threw my hands up in the air and wailed, "Oh, dear Father, I can't do this. I just can't. Please help me help Ma." After my cry for help, I can't say I felt filled with a sudden surge of confidence, but I did sense a flicker of hope. While I didn't really know Pa's God very well, I figured my father had established a strong enough relationship over the years that He would at least help me for Pa's sake. *Yes, God, Ma and I will get through this ordeal. It wouldn't hurt if the baby helped a little too*, I decided.

As I dashed about the kitchen, I could hear Hattie upstairs quieting the younger children, whose sleep had been disturbed. I grabbed a clean washcloth, filled Ma's porcelain wash basin with cool water, and carried it to the bedside. I found her writhing in pain. I couldn't bear to see my mother suffering. Tears streamed down my face as I rinsed the sweat from her forehead and face. "Don't worry, Ma. Joe will be back with Auntie Gert in no time at all, you'll see." My words sounded hollow, even to me.

"It's too late!" she cried out in agony. "It's too late!"

I wanted to run, to hide, but I couldn't. For the first time in my life, Pa, Riley, Myrtle, Hattie, and Joe couldn't help her. My mother had only me. She needed me; she depended on me. Terrified I'd make some irreversible mistake, I recited aloud the directions she'd given me, all the while trying to comfort Ma. In spite of my fear, at some point in the delivery, my actions seemed to feel almost instinctive, natural.

Finally lusty squalls filled the air as I held my slippery newborn sister in my hands. Indignation filled her scrunched-up face. I laughed as she waved her arms and kicked strong little legs. The more she kicked, the harder

I laughed, all the while sniffing back tears of relief. She was alive, and so was my mother. Shouting above the infant's squalls, I lifted her heavenward.

"A healthy baby girl—thank You, Father, thank You!"

When I heard Ma's weak laughter, I remembered that my task was not yet completed. I don't know how she did it, but Ma patiently guided me through the rest of the birthing process. As I carried out her instructions, my attention kept wandering to the tiny, flannel-wrapped bundle by her side. I was sure I'd never seen anything so beautiful, so perfectly formed as that precious girl-child.

"What are you going to call her, Ma?" I asked as I gathered up the soiled linen to take to the back porch.

"Your pa and I chose the name Dorothy Estelle, after his great aunt." My mother glanced down and held out a pinkie finger to the infant. The baby wrapped her little fist around her finger and tried to draw it into her mouth. "However, if it's all right with him," Ma looked up at me, her eyes glistening with tears, "I'd like to name her Dorothy, after his aunt and Mae, after you."

I bit my lip and nodded. "I'd like that, Ma." I'd never felt as close to my mother as I did at that moment. Maybe our natures were too different—maybe too similar, I didn't know which—but we always seemed to be at odds. Pa said I'd inherited Ma's Irish temper and his Scottish stubbornness.

I deposited the bundle of linens on the canning shelf on the back porch and hurried upstairs. Hattie would be waiting to hear the news. I tiptoed up to our bedroom. "It's a girl, a baby girl," I whispered. "Her name is Dorothy Mae. She's beautiful, utterly beautiful. She has big blue eyes and a shock of bright red—"

I stopped midsentence. For the first time I realized I hadn't even considered the color of the baby's hair. I put my hand to my mouth to suppress my laughter. "Dorothy has red hair. Isn't that amazing?"

Delighted with my discovery, I hugged Hattie and hurried back downstairs. My mother had drifted off to sleep. Her lips curved upward into a gentle smile, replacing the earlier lines of agony. A hint of blush highlighted her delicately carved cheekbones. For the first time in my sixteen years, I saw her as a young girl instead of an overworked housewife and mother.

The infant squirmed in the crook of her arm. As I reached for the baby, my mother's eyes opened slowly. "Would you like me to hold Dorothy so you can rest?"

Ma smiled and nodded. Reverently, I took the baby into my arms, walked over to Ma's mahogany rocker, and sat down.

The sleeping infant nestled against me. I couldn't believe how perfectly the tiny bundle fit in my arms. As natural as breathing, I began to rock and hum a lullaby. The words soon followed.

"Hush, little baby, don't say a word; Papa's gonna buy you a mockingbird . . ." The lullaby affected me in the same way it did my newborn sister. I closed my eyes for a moment and felt someone lifting Dorothy out of my arms. My eyes flew open. "No."

"Shh, it's all right, Chloe Mae. It's just me." Pa's six-foot frame towered over me. Joe stood behind him in the doorway. Auntie Gert stood on the opposite side of the bed, her face flushed with happiness. Suddenly I realized my work was done. Grown-ups were there to take over. I sighed with relief. "Oh, Pa, I'm so glad you're home. I was so scared—"

"Shh, your mama needs her sleep. Why don't you come out to the kitchen and tell us all about it? Auntie Gert says you did a fine job."

I followed the three of them from the room. Before my

parents' bedroom door had closed behind me, Auntie
Gert clapped her gnarled hands with delight. "Praise
God! He has answered my prayer! Now I can rest in
peace."

Pa nodded. "Yes, it looks like He has answered your
prayer, old friend." My father went on to explain that
arthritis made midwifery increasingly difficult for the
seventy-five-year-old woman. He paused and eyed me
curiously, then turned to Auntie Gert. "Would you be
willing to train Chloe, kind of as an apprentice? The
child's got a good head on her shoulders."

The woman's eyes danced with enthusiasm. "If she is
willing to learn."

Everyone looked my way. "I-I-I guess so . . ." I went to
bed that night uncertain of what I might have gotten
myself into.

A few days later, when Pa discussed Auntie Gert's
offer with Ma, she demurred. She believed that a girl
my age shouldn't be delivering babies or even be knowl-
edgeable of the process of childbirth until after marriage. Yet, she freely admitted that I had a genuine gift
of comfort and healing. After thinking about it a couple
of weeks, Ma reluctantly gave her permission.

I began accompanying Auntie Gert when she attended deliveries, and found I enjoyed being her assistant.

When school opened in the fall, my mother decided it
would be best if I didn't attend. As Ma explained,
mothers would feel it unseemly for me to attend classes
with their sons and daughters during the day and
deliver their "young-uns" at night.

I missed my friends. Pa tried to make up for my loss
by allowing time whenever we went into town for me to
go to the library for books to read. Each day after work,
he'd pick me up at Auntie Gert's. On the ride home, he

not only shared his ideas on local and national events, but encouraged me to voice my own opinions too. Usually they echoed his.

Heavy gray clouds blotted out the sun as Pa and I headed home one Monday evening. I tightened my woolen scarf about my neck and face, then burrowed deeper into my coat. Overhead, a flock of geese disappeared over the southern horizon. I sighed. "Looks like Indian summer's over for this year."

Pa grunted. "Probably so. I suppose those Yukon prospectors have given it up for winter by now." For the last several months the newspapers had reported tales of the fabulous caches of gold found in the Yukon Territory.

Pa stared off into the distance. "Yep, they called it 'Seward's folly.'" A glint of adventure flashed in his eyes. "Sure would like to get me a grubstake and head north."

I listened as he spun his dreams of life in the frozen northland. *Imagine growing up in the land of the midnight sun—living in a snow house and eating walrus blubber. Eaugh!* My imagination halted at that thought.

"Maybe next spring . . ." His voice drifted off into the silence of knowing that his roots sank too deeply in the Pennsylvania soil for him to do much more than dream.

Eager to maintain the moment of magic he'd created, I voiced my own fantasy. "Oh, Pa, when I grow up, I'm going to travel all over the world. I want to see everything there is to see."

He chuckled into his bushy red beard. "You have the heart of an explorer, Chloe Mae. Too bad you were born female."

I cocked my head to one side. "What does being a girl have to do with traveling?"

As he halted the team in front of our house, Patches

bounded around the house. Pa glanced toward me and smiled sadly. "A woman was made to serve her husband and to bear his children. That's God's plan." His tone of genuine regret fueled my zeal.

"Well, it's not my plan. I don't mind delivering babies, but I sure don't intend to bear any of my own."

Twelve-year-old Amby raced from the house as Pa helped me down off the buckboard. "Unharness the team, son."

My father draped his arm over my shoulders and sighed. His sigh rankled me further. I pulled away from his touch.

"How can you be so out of date? We're living on the brink of the twentieth century. Four states already have granted women the right to vote. In no time at all, the rest of the country will follow suit—you said so yourself."

He shook his head and walked up the steps to the porch. "Chloe Mae, it's going to take more than the right to vote to change the course of history."

I stormed past him into the house. Tugging my bonnet off my crown of braids, I tossed it onto an empty peg behind the door. I thundered up the stairs with a parting prophecy. "You wait; you'll see. I'm not going to spend the rest of my life chasing after a passel of kids—female or not!"

"Chloe?" Hattie stood beside the table, slicing a loaf of fresh bread for supper. By the stove Ma dished out the boiled potatoes onto a platter.

I threw myself onto my bed and buried my face in a down pillow. In spite of the pillow, I heard the front door slam and my mother greet my father. "What bee got into Chloe's bonnet?"

I thought, *Ah, she'll understand. She's a woman; she'll set him straight.*

Instead, when she heard his answer, she snapped at him. "Serves you right, Joseph Riley Spencer. I've been telling you all along not to fill her head with world events and—and all that man stuff. How did you expect her to react?" Ma continued to sputter. "You've allowed her to read and to learn things far beyond her station in life. You've applauded the appalling behavior of those insufferable suffragettes." I could hear dishes slamming and cooking utensils clanging about the kitchen.

My father's soothing tones drifted up the stairs. "Now, Annie, don't get your Irish up. When the time comes, she'll know her God-given place and fill it admirably."

"Humph! Well, that time isn't so far off, you know! Remember, she turns seventeen in August. And if your rule was good enough for Riley and good enough for Myrtle, and now for Joe, it must apply to your precious Chloe as well!" The back door slammed. My brothers thundered in from doing the evening chores, ending my parents' discussion.

The aroma of gravy simmering on the back burner coaxed me back downstairs. The look of defiance on my face went unnoticed when Joe burst into the house. He shed his coat and hung it on the empty peg beside my bonnet. "Looks like a storm's brewin'. Could have snow by mornin'. Hey, what's up?"

Ma set the platter of potatoes in the center of the table with a thud and narrowed her eyes toward Pa. "Nothing! Absolutely nothing!"

Clearing his throat, Pa strode over to Ma and planted a kiss on her cheek. "Remember what the Pennsylvania Dutch say, son. 'Kissin' don't last; cookin' do.' And your ma sure knows a lot about good cookin'! So let's say we enjoy some of it while it's hot."

We took our places about the table. Pa opened the Spencer family Bible that his parents had brought from

Scotland. The mantel clock ticked off the minutes while Pa searched for a verse to read. When he finally began to read, I recognized the passage instantly and sank lower into my chair, my arms tightly folded across my chest.

"Who can find a virtuous woman? for her price is far above rubies." He read all the rest of Proverbs 31. Out of the corner of my eye, I could see determination on my mother's face. While my younger brothers and little sister wriggled with impatience and Hattie fidgeted with her fork, Joe frowned, his face wreathed with confusion.

After the blessing, the usual banter of the dinner table replaced the earlier tension. The storm inside the farmhouse subsided, while outside, the first snowflakes of the season drifted past the kitchen window. By the time we'd each devoured a serving of apple cobbler, the topic was forgotten.

Babies Aplenty

Once the force of winter set in, so did Auntie Gert's arthritis, making it difficult for her to leave the warmth of her kitchen. I would sit beside her as she described some of the problems in a difficult delivery.

"Your biggest problem, Chloe, is going to be dealing with your losses. Perhaps that's where your mother is right. You are too young to face the fact that, sooner or later, you will face death." The old woman sighed and rubbed the fingers of her left hand. "The mystery of life is seldom far from the reality of death. And I have no easy answers except for what I find in the Good Book. If you search them out for yourself, God's promises will mean more to you."

I smiled and nodded, knowing that's what Auntie Gert expected of me. My parents had always taught me to respect my elders. The first week of December, Auntie Gert announced that my midwifery training was over. I was on my own.

I soon learned that the worse the weather or the more tired I felt, the more likely it would be that some baby in the county would insist on being born. When a call for help came, Pa would hitch the horses to the wagon, or the cutter, if the roads were covered with snow, and we would head for the neighbors' farmhouse to bring a new life into the world. Our patients paid Pa with sacks of potatoes, chickens, eggs, occasionally a side of beef—whatever they could afford. I liked knowing that my efforts contributed to the family food supply.

While I missed Auntie Gert, there was so much to learn about the entire healing process. I spent each evening with Pa, learning which herbs cured which ailments and which ones eased the symptoms. We worked side by side, grinding up herbs for potions and elixirs. Up in the herb room and while on house calls, he treated me differently—more as an adult than a child. Soon he took me along on all his medical calls.

The biting winds of January increased the bouts with chest colds and pneumonia throughout the community. As the winter intensified, we talked less about politics and more about our patients and their problems.

The subzero temperatures in February didn't limit the community's need to socialize. Our recreation centered around the school and the county grange hall. When the town's only church, the Community Methodist church, burned down in 1895, a few of the families took to meeting in the grange hall. My parents attended whenever a circuit-riding preacher arrived because Pa didn't appreciate Mr. Haney's long-winded sermons. My favorite was the Baptist preacher. He really knew how to sing.

Each winter the people of Shinglehouse talked about building another, but with the country in the middle of a depression, most families lacked the necessary funds to keep food on the table and the mortgages paid on the farms. So building a new church stalled at the discussion stage.

Taffy pulls, sledding, and ice-skating parties filled our social calendars. At these parties, a predictable social pattern could be expected. The men stood at one end of the hall discussing the best seed for field corn or the coming threat of war with Spain, while the women gathered beside the refreshment table and gossiped, sharing recipes and sure-fire methods of toilet training a toddler. The teenage boys posed and strutted for the teenage girls from opposite sides of the room, and the younger children ran about the hall, screaming and tripping up the older folks.

Due to my newly acquired adult status as a midwife, the girls I'd grown up with were in awe of me, and the boys my own age shied away from me. They were replaced by Riley's friends, who kept my mug filled with hot apple cider and my hands with butter cookies. While Hattie always started out by my side, I didn't notice at what point she would drift away from our group to join the older women. But I heard about it the moment we reached home.

"Sashaying about like that in front of those boys! Chloe, what could you have been thinking?" *Sashaying* was one of Ma's favorite words. In her vocabulary it could be applied to a male's actions as well as to a female's. Once she used it to describe Patches' behavior.

By the time Ma got to, "You don't see Hattie strutting about like that," all of my siblings had disappeared upstairs to their beds. After the first or second such lecture, I stopped trying to defend myself, because I had no idea what I might have done to upset her so.

Ma's sermon on the proper decorum for young ladies always included my father. "Joseph, you must do something—soon. I realize we are living in a different age. But, remember, by the time I was Chloe's age, I already had Riley, and the twins were on the way."

An early thaw postponed our socializing for more than a month and spared me a few lectures. When the roads became long quagmires, Mr. Hennessey, the town blacksmith, lent Pa his sturdy plow horses, Hans and Franz, to pull our wagon so we could continue to treat the sick.

The winter of '98 took a heavy toll on the citizens of Potter County. A number of older people didn't survive the season. Pa called the dreaded pneumonia the old man's angel of mercy. I could accept the fact that the elderly must die, but when death touched young children, I rebelled.

Though I hadn't yet lost any babies or mothers in childbirth, pneumonia claimed one of my first babies, Jeb and Mary Blackburn's infant son, Jeb junior. Harry and Lucinda Conners' baby girl died a week later. A woman over Coudersport way contracted consumption and had to go to a sanitarium in Springfield. Her husband was left with four children to raise alone.

I began to see what Auntie Gert meant about the fine line between life and death. One moment a patient would be thrashing around from a raging fever, and the next minute, stone silent. Too often, as I held a patient erect so he or she could gasp for another breath, I would pray in vain. My prayers couldn't seem to penetrate the heavy clouds hovering over our valley.

When Pa told me, "We were lucky this winter, what with the influenza epidemic running rampant in Pittsburgh and Harrisburg," I thought to myself, *Lucky? Tell that to the Conners or the Blackburns.*

At night, as my sisters slept, I would stare into the shrouded world beyond my bedroom window and demand answers. Yet, for all of my demands, no voice spoke to me, no answers came.

The day after four-year-old Corey Hanson died with whooping cough, I confronted my parents with my doubts. Pa looked up from his newspaper and frowned. "Like it or not, death's a part of life, my child."

Ma's knitting needles clicked as she rattled off her reply. "The Lord gave, and the Lord hath taken away; blessed be the name of the Lord." The words rolled off her tongue in what seemed to me to be careless abandon.

"Ma, how can you say that? What if we were talking about Dorothy instead of Corey Hanson?" I shuddered. Of the infants I'd delivered, none was more beautiful or more precious to me than my little sister Dorothy.

Ma glanced up from the blue sweater she was knitting and tapped her thickening waist. "You'll learn. There'll always be another."

Horrified, I whirled about and ran up the stairs to my room. How could she imply that one child could take the place of another? Did she think so little about each of us, her children? I pushed the frightening thoughts from my mind. A few minutes later, Pa called me out to the herb room to help him make a new potion for Auntie Gert's arthritis.

As I stood beside him, grinding the garlic cloves with his marble pestle, Pa measured out the dried herbs he would need for the potion. Only after he scraped the herbs into the small marble bowl did he refer to my mother's words.

"Don't be too hard on her, Chloe. Remember, she's miscarried three times. She laid a boy child in the grave before ever having held him in her arms. And with each loss, she grieved."

I shook my head. "Then how can she be so cold about the death of another woman's child?"

"Some things in life you have to learn to accept. Death is one of them." Tears filled his eyes. Silently, he wrapped his arm about me and pulled me to him. He held me close for some time. Finally, he spoke. "It's just your ma's way of dealing with her own demons." His voice grew heavy with emotion. "This young-un she's carrying—it came along too soon after Dorothy. Something's not right, and your ma's afraid."

A cold draft blew through the cracks in the wall. I wrapped my arms about myself to ward off a sudden, icy chill. *Will this winter never end?*

I went to bed one night in the cold of winter and awoke in the morning to the magic of spring green. In a matter of days, my drab little world of gray and brown sprang to life. Whenever possible, I escaped the confines of the house to discover springtime's latest surprise. A gentle green carpet covered the hillside beyond the swollen creek. Warm breezes forced the redbud and dogwood trees to compete for attention.

It was on such a day that I first encountered Emmett Sawyer. Though we'd never met, I'd overheard the town gossips talking about him and his fourteen-year-old son Charley in Haney's Mercantile. He was said to be from over Wellsville way; his wife, Sadie, was said to have died of influenza.

One glance out the window on the sunny May afternoon, and I knew it was a perfect day to wash my hair. Washing a head of hair as thick and as long as mine was a major undertaking. The drying process took hours; and the hair had to be dry by bedtime.

After rinsing my hair a second time, I wrapped a towel about my head, grabbed my hairbrush, and went out onto the front porch. A black-and-white blur raced around the corner of the house and leaped up on my skirt.

"Patches! Get down. Your paws are muddy." The dog slunk away to the barnyard. I removed the towel and shook my hair free. A long, tangled mass of burnished curls tumbled down over my shoulders and back. I flipped my hair from side to side to hasten the drying process. The wet strands responded to my persistence and to the warm afternoon sun as I brushed out the snarls. Tired of sitting, I skipped down the porch steps and whirled about on the small patch of grass in front of our house. The breeze rippling through my untamed mane felt lovely. I seemed so free, so alive—like a little girl. My skirts tangled about my ankles in protest.

I don't know whether it was the sunshine or my own impish nature that lured me down to the creek. But once I gazed into the crystal water of the creek bed, I knew what I must do. Strands of hair, unaccustomed to the freedom, swirled about my face as I sat down on the exposed elm root and undid my high-button shoes. I didn't want to think about the tangle I would later have to brush. I pushed my hair back over my shoulders and removed my black woolen stockings.

Lifting my skirts to my knees, I stepped off the bank into the shoals. The icy waters inched up to my ankles, then to my calves. I squealed with delight. Mud squished between my toes. Within seconds, I was splashing about in total abandon. Ma would have been horrified.

Suddenly, as if the sun had dipped behind a cloud, a chill skittered up my spine. Sensing I wasn't alone, I whirled about. A lone rider on horseback sat by the road, watching and laughing. My hands flew to my flushed face, then back to my now sodden skirts. Indignant, I leaped from the water and hid behind the trunk of the elm. The stranger laughed again and headed down the road.

Of all the nerve, I thought. *A gentleman would have pretended not to see me.* One of Ma's reprimands came to mind: "A lady would not have allowed herself to be caught in such a compromising situation."

Once I was certain he'd gone, I came out of hiding. I

snaked my fingers through my tangled locks and tried to weave them into a semblance of braids. Tying a sprig of grass around the ends of the braids to keep them from unraveling, I danced about the moss at the base of the tree, scrubbing the mud from my toes. If I hurried home in time to help Ma prepare supper, no one would ever need to know how foolish I'd been.

I dashed across the grassy slope and into the back-yard. Pausing at the slat fence, I wrung out the hem of my skirt and petticoats, adjusted the apron over my skirt, opened the gate, and ran into the house.

The door to the pantry had barely closed behind me when I realized it was later than I imagined. I heard Pa's voice and that of a stranger. A sense of foreboding nibbled at the corners of my mind. Ma must have heard the back door slam. "Chloe, is that you? Please bring me two spuds from the bin."

I chose two potatoes and squared my shoulders before entering the kitchen. *This is my home,* I thought. *I will not enter it like a stray field mouse!* I pushed the dividing door open and crossed to the stove, where Ma stood slicing a large russet potato into a frying pan. "Here, Ma, will these two do?"

My hands shook as I handed her the potatoes.

"Whatever happened to you? Your hair is a mess," she hissed. Composing myself as best I could, I smiled and walked over to where Hattie sat rocking Dorothy. "She's fast asleep. Would you like me to carry her to her cradle?"

"Wait, Chloe." Pa strode to my side and wrapped his arm about my shoulders. "I would like to introduce you to Emmett Sawyer. Emmett, this is my daughter, Chloe Mae. And Chloe Mae, this is Mr. Sawyer."

Our eyes met, and I knew my life was over. For a couple of seconds I thought I would die of humiliation right there in front of my parents. But my discomfort quickly switched to anger. My right hand itched to wipe that smug little grin from his face. Clutching his hat in both hands, the middle-aged farmer tipped his head toward me and pursed his lips.

"How nice to meet you, Miss Chloe. I look forward to getting to know you better in the days to come—if and when our paths cross."

I smiled the smile of a dutiful daughter, nodded my head in polite deference, then glared. The man took a step backward in surprise.

"If and when our paths cross, of course, Mr. Sawyer. Now, if you'll excuse me, I need to help Ma finish supper."

Over the next three weeks, I ran into the man everywhere I went—at the mercantile, at grange meetings, in front of Minnie Perkins' dress shop. Even when I stayed home, he showed up at our door, asking to see my father.

While I noticed the curious glances passing between my parents, I failed to see any significance until the all-day meeting at the grange. For weeks, posters announcing the visit of Pastor and Mrs. Victor Van Dorn, missionaries from China, appeared in every storefront in town. The advertisement said that the Van Dorns were touring the United States to raise money for their mission work in Canton. They would have genuine Chinese artifacts, including photographs of the people and their country.

In the remote hamlet of Shinglehouse, where all entertainment was home-grown, a visiting missionary ranked right up there with a religious revival meeting or a traveling circus. Everyone would be there, from Hector, the town drunk, to the Chamberlains, the town royalty.

On the appointed Sunday, Ma had a bout of morning sickness and decided not to go. Pa agreed to take us only after Hattie and I promised to manage the younger children. After morning chores, we packed a picnic lunch and headed for town. Hattie led the way into the grange while I herded the children from the rear.

Mr. Haney, owner of the mercantile, introduced the speaker. From his first words, Pastor Van Dorn held all of us spellbound. His tales of the exotic Orient and the devastating needs of the people there wrenched tears from our eyes and coins from our pocketbooks. Even Josiah Goodwin, the town atheist, who trumpeted the teachings of the French philosopher Voltaire, dropped a coin into the offering plate.

At noon, the women of the community unpacked their choicest casseroles, pies, and cakes from their picnic baskets onto the sawhorse tables on the front lawn of the grange. As I stood looking for a place to set Ma's Dutch oven of chicken 'n' dumplings, Emmett Sawyer stepped up to my side. "My, you sure look purty in that blue gingham dress, Miss Chloe. And those dumplings smell somethin' good."

I smiled a weak smile and inched away. He pursued. In desperation, I insinuated myself between two of the women standing near the center of the table.

"Excuse me, please, got a hot kettle here." They made room for me. I placed the pot and the hot pad on the table. "Thank you," I murmured, "mighty heavy."

Turning toward the woman on my left, I smiled. "Mrs. Peterson, what a lovely gabardine frock. The rose tone accentuates your natural ivory complexion so beautifully. You must have ordered it from New York City."

The young woman twisted her head from side to side and patted her Gibson girl hairdo. Then as if confiding a choice bit of gossip, she leaned forward. "Why, Chloe

Mae, I must be honest with you. I copied it from one I saw in the Monkey Ward catalog. I used the fabric from one of my mother's hoop-skirted dresses, rest her soul."

I peered over her shoulder at the retiring figure of Mr. Sawyer and returned my attention to the dress. "Well, I am impressed. Before we know it, you'll be giving poor Minnie Perkins a little competition."

Mrs. Peterson giggled behind her hand, then waved me away. "Oh, no, dear, I could never . . ."

I patted her arm. "Well, it is a lovely dress, Mrs. Peterson." I glanced over her shoulder once more to be certain Mr. Sawyer had disappeared from view. "Oh, no, will you excuse me? My little brother Worley is giving Hattie fits and commotions."

I slipped between two of the men waiting in the food line and ran to the far side of the lawn, where Hattie had spread out a blanket. Worley sat with legs crossed and lips pouting while his baby sister lay asleep on one corner of the blanket. "Hattie, let me take Worley over to Amby and Jesse. It won't hurt them to watch him for a while, at least while we eat. I'll watch Dorothy while you get yourself a plate of food."

When I returned from my errand and dropped onto the blanket, Hattie struggled to her feet and limped over to the food line. I closed my eyes. The sounds of laughter and the warmth of sunlight filled my mind with peace.

In sharp contrast to the euphoria I felt, lurid pictures of starving, diseased people paraded through my mind. Mothers and newborns dying without medical help. Children suffering from blood poisoning. I could hear Mr. Van Dorn's booming bass voice relating the physical and spiritual needs of these forgotten people.

"And the Master said unto them, 'Go ye into all the world, and preach the gospel to every creature.' That, my friends, includes the untold millions of Chinese who live and die without hearing the very name of Jesus."

With the suddenness of a lightning bolt, I knew. An icy tingle ran up my spine. *China—God wants me to go as a missionary to China.* I had never been particularly religious. For all the books I'd read, I'd never considered reading the Bible. Pa was the one who read the Bible at the table and offered a blessing before each meal. Sometimes I'd seen him late in the evening, sitting beside the kitchen stove, reading from God's Word. No, religion was Pa's job, not mine.

I'd never heard of God directing anyone to go to a foreign land. I tried to shake the conviction growing inside me. But the more I denied it, the stronger it grew. When Hattie returned with her food, I made my way over to the group of women surrounding Annabelle Van Dorn. They were asking questions. When the missionary finished answering one of the women's question, I interrupted.

"Excuse me, Mrs. Van Dorn, but what do I have to do to become a missionary to China?" The woman smiled at me as she would at a precocious ten-year-old. I continued, hoping I could convince her that I was serious. "God just told me He wants me to go to China, and I have no idea how to go about it." I knew I sounded petulant, but I refused to waver.

The surrounding women stared at me as if I'd just arrived from China instead of having proposed going. Mrs. Van Dorn cleared her throat. "Well, child, it would be very difficult for a young woman like yourself to travel alone to China. My advice to you would be, find a good man who shares your conviction."

"I-I-I don't want—"

The missionary patted me gently on the shoulder and suggested, "Make it a matter of prayer, dear."

"But-I-I—"

Sensing my frustration, she added, "Mark my words, child. If God wants you to go as a missionary to China, He will work it out."

I don't know exactly what I'd expected her to say, but that was hardly it. I wanted specific directions. I turned and walked away. I needed time to think, to be alone. I strolled over to a grassy knoll behind the grange hall and sat down. In the distance, I could hear Mr. Haney announce the beginning of the afternoon session. I knew I should go back and help Hattie round up the boys, but at that moment, I didn't care. I hugged my knees and rested my chin on my forearm.

"Dear heavenly Father, I'm so confused." I hoped I was doing it right, talking so directly, but it had worked the evening Dorothy was born. "I really did believe You spoke to me back there on the lawn. Now, I'm not so sure."

I didn't hear footsteps approaching until the intruder spoke. "Is this a private party, or may I join you?"

I twisted about, fire leaping from my eyes. "Mr. Sawyer, what do I have to do to convince you—" I stopped midsentence and blushed.

Shock filled Phillip Chamberlain's face. "I-I-I truly am sorry. I-I-I didn't mean to interrupt anything."

I reached up toward him. "Oh, no. I'm so sorry. I thought you were someone else."

He breathed a low whistle and shook his head. "I'm mighty glad I'm not whoever you thought I was. The fire in your eyes could slay a mountain lion."

I laughed. "Please, sit down if you'd like. I really don't mind."

He dropped onto the knoll beside me, allowing a comfortable space between us. "So what do you think of this Van Dorn person?"

After the women's reaction to my announcement, I wondered how honest I should be. Should I play the coquette, flirt, say all the right things—or should I risk being me? I chose to be me.

"I can't imagine a greater commission than to be sent as a missionary." My voice was heavy with emotion.

"Really?" He acted pleasantly surprised. My words tumbled over one another as I tried to explain myself, but he stopped me.

"Don't apologize, I know how you feel. Last fall, I attended similar lectures at Harvard and decided to become a missionary to Africa. I was serious enough to change my major from law to theology." He paused and inhaled slowly. "When my father came East to bail Cy, my older brother, out of trouble, Dad exploded all over the back bay. And as a result, he brought us both back to Shinglehouse with him."

Sympathy welled up inside me. I glanced over at him. But he didn't notice. His attention was focused on some distant point along the horizon. I waited for him to continue speaking. When he remained silent, I wondered if I should say something. Since I'd never been good at small talk, I waited. Five minutes or more passed. Suddenly, he shook his head as if drawing himself back to the present. The painful smile he gave me conveyed more than any words he could have spoken.

"I don't know why I'm telling you this. I hardly know you." He picked a blade of grass and nibbled it. "Sometimes I think I disappointed my parents more for wanting to be a minister than my brother did for being expelled from school for cheating."

"And what now?"

He shrugged his shoulders. "Mr. Rockefeller promised my father he would find positions for both Cy and me. Railroads, oil, banking—I don't know. And I guess I really don't care." Suddenly his face brightened. "Enough of my woes; tell me, what's there to do in a small town like Shinglehouse?"

I rolled my eyes heavenward. "We have a nice little library. And there's always the latest gossip, both local and national."

"Oh?"

"Why, yes, did you know that George, the town barber, is courting Miss Bladkin? She lives in Coudersport. And did you hear about the assistant secretary of the United States Navy's slur against President McKinley? Mr. Roosevelt said the president has as much backbone as a chocolate eclair! By the way, what's a chocolate eclair?"

Phillip tipped his head back and laughed. "A French pastry filled with air and whipped cream." I asked him questions about the cities he'd visited—Boston, Philadelphia, and Pittsburgh. I'd never enjoyed an afternoon so much in my life. When the pump organ inside the grange hall wheezed out the opening chords of "Rescue the Perishing," we stared at one another. The afternoon meeting wasn't beginning, it was over.

Phillip leaped up, took my hands in his, and helped me to my feet. He stared down at my hands still trapped in his. Reluctantly, he released them. I felt an immediate loss. "You are so easy to talk to, Miss Spencer. I hate to let you go." He brushed invisible specks from his trousers. "I hope I haven't upset your father by keeping you out here like this during the meeting."

I groaned and rolled my eyes heavenward. "I'll hear about it, I'm sure. But you didn't keep me out here. I was here first, remember?"

He glanced first one direction, then the other. A group of young boys stood talking over by the wagons.

With a dimpled smile and a teasing wink, he suggested, "If I head around the other side of the building and slip into the back row of the hall, no one will need to know we played hooky from the afternoon meeting."

He disappeared around the corner of the gray stone building. I waited until the congregation started the last verse of the hymn, then strolled over to a bench in the side yard and sat down.

In a few minutes, people began emerging from the hall and hurrying to their wagons. Because most were farmers, they had cows to milk before the daylight disappeared. Hattie looked at me questioningly as I joined our family and helped her herd the children into the wagon. Pa strode over to the wagon and climbed into the driver's seat. "Hattie! Joe! You two ride in back with the young-uns. Chloe Mae, you sit up here with me!"

At the edge of town, the back wheels of the wagon cleared the bridge's surface before Pa spoke. "Chloe Mae, I have never been as angry with you as I am at this moment. If you were a few years younger, I'd give you the strapping of your life. I might anyway!" He snapped the reins across the team's back. The wagon lurched forward.

I swallowed hard. "Pa—"

He held up one finger before my face. "Don't say anything. If I had known you were out there with the Chamberlain boy . . ." Tears sprang up in my eyes. The last thing I would ever want to do was disappoint my father.

"Pa, we were just talking, honest." I hastened on before he could reply. "Did you know that Phillip wants to be a minister and go as a missionary to Africa? Isn't that exciting?"

"Humph! The day his parents allow him to do that!"

We rode for a few minutes without speaking. If I were going to share my newfound conviction with my father, I knew I'd better do it while I had him alone. Besides, if I could get him talking about the day's events, he might forget his anger at me.

"And, Pa, that's not all. After listening to Pastor Van Dorn describe the desperate conditions in China today, I would love to go too."

"Huh?" My father glanced toward me. He hadn't heard what I said. "Where was that you want to go, Chloe Mae?"

I sucked in my breath. "I want to become a missionary to China. I honestly believe that God . . ."

My father shook his head. "Chloe Mae, you come up with the wildest ideas sometimes. Most girls your age dream of riding off into the sunset with their knight in shining armor." He frowned. "I think your mother may be right. I've treated you too much like a son instead of a daughter—perhaps, it's not too late to rectify the situation."

I scowled as I replied, "I-I-I don't understand."

The worry lines on his face deepened. "We'll finish this conversation this evening after the young-uns are asleep."

"But, Pa . . ." My protests failed to penetrate the wall of silence he'd constructed between us.

The Marryin' Mood

What did I say? What did I do? Every now and then, I stole a glance at his granite-chiseled profile. When we arrived home, Pa handed the reins to Joe and strode into the house.

I stepped inside the kitchen in time to see him usher Ma into their bedroom. Now, I knew there was trouble. My parents never retreated to the privacy of their bedroom except at bedtime or for a powwow, as Pa called it. Without a word, Amby and Jesse changed into their work clothes and headed for the barn. Hattie rushed about the kitchen, starting supper. Only Ori and Dorothy didn't recognize the signs of the coming fury.

The chores were done and supper ready before my parents emerged from the bedroom. Ma's eyes were red and puffy. Silently, we gathered about the table and waited for Pa to read from the Bible. Instead, he growled, "Well, what are you waiting for? Eat!"

We looked at one another, then timidly obeyed. When Worley grumbled about the large chunks of onions in his potato salad, Pa ordered him to bed without supper. Bewildered, my brother climbed the stairs to his room. I knew I'd caused the trouble, not him. He didn't deserve to go to bed hungry. I turned toward my father. "Pa, it's not fair—"

Before I could finish my sentence, I found myself staring down the tines of my father's fork. "Chloe Mae, not another word!"

Our eyes met and held. His eyes revealed a procession of conflicting emotions—anger, sadness, love, frustration, followed by a mist of tears. He cleared his throat and stared at his plate of food.

A lump that felt the size of Ma's unbaked bread dough formed in my throat. I nibbled at my supper. One by one the rest of the family gulped down their food and excused themselves. When I asked to be excused, Pa growled, "You stay right where you are."

Hattie filled a kettle of water for dishes and set it on the stove, then removed the children's empty plates from the table. When she reached for Ma's bowl, Ma placed her hand on my sister's wrist. "Just stack the dirty dishes beside the dishpan, Hattie. And if you could settle Dorothy down for the night, I'd appreciate it."

Hattie glanced toward Pa, then toward me. "Yes, ma'am."

I took the stack of dishes from Hattie's hands. "You just go ahead with Dorothy; I'll do these." I carried the dishes to the wet sink and rinsed them under the spout of the hand pump. As Hattie hobbled across the kitchen toward our parents' bedroom, I wanted to shout, "Hurry! Don't you see Ma and Pa are waiting for you to leave before yelling at me," but I didn't. For as much as I wanted to get it over with, I ached to bolt out the back door and up to my hiding place in the barn.

I puttered about at the sink, glancing every few seconds at the copper hands of the mantel clock. The seconds ticked away. Five minutes or fifteen, I don't know how long it was before Hattie came out from the bedroom, kissed Ma and Pa goodnight, then climbed the stairs to our room. At the sound of my sister's feet on the landing, I squared my shoulders and walked over to my place at the table. I placed my hands on the back of my chair.

"Well?" I looked at my mother. She, in turn, glared at my father. I gazed at him as he sat studying his gnarled hands, folded on the table before him. "Well?"

He inhaled deeply and untangled his fingers. "You'd better sit down, Chloe Mae. Your ma and I have made an important decision." Pa reached across the dark-stained table and placed his hand on mine. "Chloe, your ma and I've been talkin'. We're right pleased with the handsome and strong young woman you've become. And except for your temper, and perhaps your impetuous behavior—" He cleared his voice and glanced at my mother before continuing. "And except for your temper, any man in his right mind would consider himself lucky to have you for a wife."

What is he getting at? I shot a look in my mother's direction. She sat knitting in the rocker beside the fireplace, carefully avoiding my gaze. Her knitting needles flew, revealing the emotions her passive face masked. I turned back to my father, fury rising inside me. "A wife? It sounds like you're describing a work-horse or a prize heifer!"

Pa chuckled a nervous little laugh and patted my hand. "Now, Chloe, hear us out. As a father, I believe it's my obligation before God to start each of you children out right in this world." He paused to clear his throat. "I've done the same for each of the others and will do no less for you."

"I don't understand what is happening here. I thought you were upset because I missed the afternoon meeting."

Ma's words came out shrilly. "And that's another—"

"Now, Annie, we agreed, I'd do the explainin' here."
Pa's low, even tone halted my mother midsentence. She
clamped her mouth shut and set the chair to rocking
and needles to clacking at a faster pace. My father
continued. "There comes a time when grown children
should set out on their own. Nature intended for sons to
find jobs and for daughters to marry."

"Pa, I don't want to get married right now, and I'm
already working, delivering babies and helping Ma here
at the house. Isn't that enough?"

Ma's eyes narrowed as she jabbed her knitting
needles in my direction. "You need a man and some
babies to calm you down, to make a lady out of you.
Goodness knows, I've tried. When I was your age . . ."
She glanced toward Pa, then reached for the ball of
yarn in her knitting basket. "Besides, it's a woman's
place to marry and bear children. That's what the
good Lord intended."

I chuckled aloud. "Don't these activities usually take
a cooperative male somewhere along the way? I don't
exactly have a line of beaus congregating at the front
door."

"I'm comin' to that, Chloe Mae." Pa glanced toward
Ma. Alarm bells rang in my head. My pulse rate increased. *What is he saying?*

"Seventeen is a good age for a girl to marry. Look at
your sister Myrtle. Why, she's as happy as a clam in a
half shell."

I arched one eyebrow and mumbled, "A clam in a half
shell is dead."

My mother's hands flew into the air. "See? I tried to
warn you, Joseph. Thanks to you, she's too opinionated.
She needs a husband who will exert a firm hand over
her!"

I remembered my twenty-year-old sister sleeping

upstairs. "Hattie's not married yet. She seems to be doing fine without a husband and his firm hand!"

My father shook his head sadly. "Your sister didn't inherit a temperament like yours either. And besides, no man can afford a lame wife."

My mouth dropped open. "Pa! I can't believe you said that."

He shoved his chair back from the end of the table and rose to his feet. "It's just the way it is." His eyes misted as he ran the back of his hand along the side of my face. One glance toward Ma and he drew back his hand as if he'd touched a hot grate on the cookstove. "It's settled, Chloe Mae. I've given Emmett Sawyer permission to court you. He plans to come callin' after supper tomorrow night."

I leaped to my feet. "Emmett Sawyer? He's older than you, Pa!"

Pa averted his eyes. "It's not as if we're shipping you off to California or Timbuktu to marry a stranger. He'll woo you with flowers and sweet talk. He has been through the courtin' thing before, you know."

"The courtin' thing? Don't I have any say in this? Shouldn't I be allowed to pick out my own beau?" I searched their faces for a glimmer of compassion or understanding. For a moment, I detected a flicker of sympathy in my mother's face. I rushed to her side and knelt down in front of her. "Ma, I have dreams. I want to do something big—not be saddled down with five young-uns before I turn twenty years old."

Her face hardened. She stuffed her knitting into her knitting basket, then folded her hands on her gently protruding stomach. "If you're hoping to catch Mr. Fancy Pants Chamberlain, forget it. His hoity-toity mama plans to import his wife from Baltimore or Philadel-phia."

I arose to my feet and walked toward my father. "Is that what this is all about, my talking with Phillip this afternoon? Don't worry. It won't happen again." Exasperated, I continued, "We just talked, talked about his dream of becoming a minister, and I told him that I feel called to go as a missionary to China—that's it! I have no intention of marrying Phillip or anyone else right now."

"Chloe Mae, this isn't how I planned it—" Pa reached for my arm. His gentle touch brought tears to my eyes.

I choked them back and pulled out of his grasp. "What do you mean, planned it? How long have you been planning this? Why don't you just stand me on an auction block in front of Haney's Mercantile and have the local suitors inspect my teeth and gums before buying—"

My mother's eyes flashed with indignation. "Chloe Mae! Don't talk to your father that way."

While I knew I was balancing on the fence between anarchy and sudden destruction, I stomped my foot and whirled away from my father. "I don't want that forty-seven-year-old farmer sweet talkin' me." The kettle on the stove whistled, giving me an excuse to do something—anything. I walked over to the stove, picked up a hot pad, and grabbed the kettle. My skirt swooshed about my ankles in protest as I carried the kettle to the sink and poured the hot water into the dishpan. The steam from the boiling liquid billowed up, scalding the back of my hand. I screamed, dropped the kettle into the sink, and ran out the back door. I ignored my father's call and kept running. I could hear Ma shouting. "See? You've spoiled her. Too big for her britches. If I've told you once . . ."

As I charged out into the night, Patches appeared out of the darkness and tagged after me. Instinctively, I knew my destination. There was only one place in the world where I could find comfort.

The barn door groaned on its hinges as I hauled it open, then let it slam shut behind me. I scrambled up the wooden ladder to the loft, leaving a bewildered Patches whining at the bottom.

Moonlight streaked through the cracks between the wallboards. I'd never been alone in the herb room at night before. Instead of being warm and consoling, the room appeared cold and cavernous. I inched over to Ma's camelback trunk, then dropped onto the quilt lying on the floor behind it. As I huddled behind the trunk, I shuddered at the sound of tiny feet scurrying across the grain floor on the opposite side of the partition—mice. Even my worst nemesis couldn't frighten me back to the house tonight. I pounded on the wall. The scurrying stopped.

Hugging my knees, I rocked back and forth in agony. The peace I usually found in my private sanctuary eluded me. *How could I feel called of God this afternoon and abandoned by God a few hours later? "Honor thy father and thy mother." If I refuse to obey Pa, am I disobeying God? Or maybe God has nothing to do with it. Maybe I'm just being ornery.*

I remembered scraps of conversations I'd overheard before Myrtle's wedding day—scraps that had suddenly taken on a new, frightening meaning. I had been sitting by the bedroom window, working on a poem for Miss Hanson's English class, while Hattie and Myrtle sat on the edge of their bed, sewing a lace border along the hemline of Myrtle's russet-and-cream wedding gown.

"Pa's giving me a twenty-dollar gold piece for a wedding present. He doesn't want me going to Franklin penniless. He says he has one for each of us children, as a dowry for the girls and a nest egg for the boys—to get them started in business, you know."

I glanced up quickly. Hattie's and my eyes met. A wave of pain washed across Hattie's face. She dropped her head without a word. Myrtle rambled on, unaware of Hattie's feelings. "Yes, he gave one to Riley on his seventeenth birthday, the day before Riley left home."

And now, up here alone in the loft of the barn, other conversations I'd overheard between my parents came back to me, and the pieces fell into place like the pattern of a crazy quilt. Riley had left home the day after his seventeenth birthday. Myrtle had married on her seventeenth birthday. What about Joe? Since his seventeenth birthday, he began working for the Chamberlains. That left Hattie and me. I shuddered. I would turn seventeen in August. I wrapped one end of the old quilt about my shoulders. A winter chill still stung the spring night air.

I was in the middle of some serious wool gathering when I heard the barn door below creak. The rungs of the wooden ladder groaned under the intruder's weight. Holding my breath as if to wish myself invisible, I prayed it wouldn't be my father. I couldn't face Pa—not yet. Though I felt like a twelve-year-old for my outburst, I couldn't give in to my parents' decree. I knew that if Pa allowed Farmer Sawyer to court me, I was as good as married. In Potter County, good girls didn't dally with men's hearts.

I thought of Sylvia Farnsworth. She allowed Jim Goodwin to court her, then refused to marry him. Her reputation was forever ruined. Last I heard she had moved to Latham's Corners to care for a sick relative. She had not yet married.

The intruder reached the top of the ladder and crossed to Pa's worktable. During my last moments of solitude, I silently vowed, *I don't care what anyone says! Even if I have to remain single the rest of my days, I won't marry that forty-seven-year-old man!*

"Chloe, I know you're up here." My brother Joe struck a match against the corner of the table and lighted the wick in the kerosene lamp. Blowing out the match, he replaced the glass chimney. "You're so predictable."

He looked down at me huddled behind the trunk. "Aren't you getting a little too old to think you can solve your problems by running away and hiding in the barn?" Reaching down, he lifted me to my feet. "Chloe, you can't run away from this one. Pa means business."

Sadness mixed with love flooded through me as I looked up into my brother's troubled blue eyes. Joe avoided confrontations almost as much as I. He was the gentlest, kindest person in the world and the last person, after Pa, I'd want to hurt. I shook my head. "Joe, I mean business too. I won't marry that old man."

A pained smile touched the corners of his mouth. "You don't really have too many choices. It's not as if you can strike out on your own, you know—being a woman and all."

His argument stoked the fire in my soul. Planting my hands on my hips, I launched my debate. "How can you say that? Why, look at Susan B. Anthony. She's traveling all over the country by herself."

He thought for a moment. "Susan B. Anthony? Who's Susan B. Anthony?"

I groaned in exasperation. "Don't you read the papers? Susan B. Anthony is a suffragette. Last week she stopped in Wellsville, of all places, on her cross-country speaking tour."

Joe flexed a tiny muscle in his left cheek, the only sign he ever gave of being irritated. "You are the one who talks politics with Pa, not me." He traced a knothole on the floor with the toe of his boot. "Look, Chloe

Mae, if you're hoping to land one of the Chamberlain brothers, forget it."

I gritted my teeth. "Doesn't anyone understand? I don't want to marry Phillip Chamberlain—or anyone else—right now."

Joe folded his arms across his chest. "Well, what is it you do want to do?" He took my hands in his. "Give Emmett a chance. He might grow on you—"

"Like a wart," I mumbled.

Joe grinned and continued. "In the long run, I don't think Pa will force you to marry the man if you really can't stand the old geezer."

"Well . . ." I cocked my head to one side. "I guess we'll find out, won't we?"

We climbed down the ladder and walked out of the barn. As I walked, I thought about the day. Branded in my mind forever were thoughts of faceless young Chinese women, hardly more than children themselves, dying in the throes of childbirth. I ached to explain to my favorite brother what had happened to me that morning, but how could I? I couldn't even explain it to myself yet.

"Joe, I know this sounds strange, but I honestly believe God wants me to go to China. Should I disregard what I believe to be God's leading?"

Joe frowned and shook his head. "Look, little sister, you've never been particularly religious before you spent an hour sitting on the lawn with Phillip Chamberlain. Don't confuse religion and romance. While each may have its place in life, neither can keep food on the table or firewood in the woodshed."

I turned to face my brother. Shadows hid his expression from my view. "Why, Joe Spencer, you're a cynic!"

"No, just practical. You would be wise to follow my example. Make life easy for yourself and go along with

Pa on this Emmett thing for a while."

My jaw hardened at the repulsive idea. In the darkness of the back porch, Joe continued, "Chloe, Pa's serious about this. Don't try to buck him on it. It won't work—even for you."

Even for me? At that moment I realized what he was saying, what he'd been saying all along, and I'd been too caught up in my own problems to hear. He resented Pa's and my special relationship. How many times had Joe listened while Pa and I argued some political issue or how many evenings had he watched us ride off together on medical emergencies and felt left out? My heart reached out to him. Maybe he was right. Maybe it was time for me to grow up, to accept my womanly responsibilities.

Help me, Joe. I'm so confused. I need you. I squeezed my eyes shut, trying to erase the memory of Emmett Sawyer sitting atop his horse and laughing at me as I waded in the stream. I knew that my opinion of the man wouldn't change if he courted me for twenty-five years. On the other hand, Joe was right. As much as I hated admitting it, until I could find another solution, I would need to go along with my parents.

"Well?" He waited for my reply.

I took a deep breath and exhaled. "I'll go along with Pa for a while, but other than that, I'll make no promises."

His voice revealed his relief. "That's my wise little sister. Why make trouble for yourself? Brr! That wind is getting mighty chilly." He threw his arm around my shoulders and gave me a squeeze. "Come on, let's go inside the house." As I followed my brother into the now-silent house, I mentally retraced my steps for the day and identified my big mistake.

To understand the significance of my "crime," I must

explain the significance of the Chamberlain family. While New Yorkers revered their Vanderbilts and Massachusetts, their Cabots and their Lodges, the residents of Shinglehouse followed the lives of the Chamberlains with the undying devotion usually reserved for European royalty.

As personal friends of John D. Rockefeller, Sr., the Chamberlains had moved to Shinglehouse from Philadelphia so that Mr. Chamberlain could oversee Rockefeller's interests in the oil fields where John D. made his first million.

Every man in the county envied Cyrus Chamberlain III's matching team of Morgans, and every woman, the elegance of Mrs. Isabelle Paddington Chamberlain, of the Baltimore Paddingtons. When Mrs. Chamberlain traveled by rail to New York City for the social season, the local sales of the New York papers soared. The women in town wanted to read about the extravagant parties the lovely Isabelle attended. And when Mrs. Chamberlain returned to Shinglehouse with so much as an additional tuck or flounce to her bustle, the town dressmaker's business tripled overnight.

Chamberlain watching didn't limit itself to adults. The hearts of single females between the ages of eight and eighteen, along with their scheming mothers, palpitated dangerously the moment Cyrus IV and his younger brother, Phillip, arrived in town. Their heartbeats waned when the two boys left to attend college in Massachusetts, but revived when the boys returned home halfway through their first semester. And I myself couldn't deny the flutter or two I felt whenever Cy's dimpled grin turned my way or when I realized Phillip's serious gaze was directed at me.

Yet, for all the reverence the townspeople displayed toward the Chamberlains, an underlying current of resentment surfaced whenever a member of the "royal" family was mentioned. Yes, that had been my mistake—thinking I could hobnob, as Ma would call it, with the likes of the Chamberlains.

Relieved to learn my parents had gone to bed, I hurried upstairs to my room. I tiptoed over to the bed I shared with Ori and changed into my cambric nightgown. Sitting on the edge of the bed, I stared out at the moonlit world of light and shadows.

Yes, if I'd been talking with any other boy in town—I knew what I had to do. I would play the obedient daughter. I would avoid mentioning either Phillip or China to anyone in the family. And with a bit of Irish luck and the rush of spring planting, Emmett Sawyer would be too busy for courting until fall. By that time I could easily convince my parents to reconsider.

Trouble Comes Calling

So much for my Irish luck! The next evening, Hattie and I had barely cleared the supper dishes from the table when a knock sounded at the door. Pa went to answer it. A grinning, slicked-down man stood in the doorway, hat in hand. "Evenin', Joseph."

"And a good evenin' to you, Em." Turning toward me, Pa announced, "Chloe Mae, Mr. Sawyer is here to see you."

My little brother Worley giggled and singsonged, "Chloe's got a boyfriend." I opened my mouth, then snapped it shut. One glance at my mother, and I knew not to protest. She came up behind me and untied the apron from my waist.

"Chloe Mae, why don't you take Mr. Sawyer into the parlor while I fetch him a cup of tea." Smiling at Emmett, Ma asked, "You would like a cup of tea now, wouldn't you?"

Emmett nodded and grinned while his hands worried the rim of his hat. I forced a smile and led him into the parlor. Our parlor was the last place I wanted to be. Whenever Ma sent me in to dust, the room smothered me. Heavy, gold-brocade drapes covered the tall, narrow windows. The fireplace with its massive carved-oak mantel, dark mahogany furniture, and a faded Oriental rug added to the gloom.

The parlor lamps had already been lighted, illuminating the grim faces of three generations of Scottish and Irish kinsmen over the mantel. I invited Emmett to sit beside me on the maroon velvet sofa.

Now what, I thought, folding my hands neatly in my lap. I smiled at the nervous man by my side. Would he mention my frolic in the creek?

"It was a little cooler today. Think we're in for a cold snap?"

He stared down at his hands. "Might be."

"Well . . ." I glanced about the room. A strange pattern of light and dark shadows danced on the patterned wallpaper. "Uh, do you think we'll win the war with Spain?"

"Don't know; don't care."

Ma bustled into the room with a tea tray, which she set on the marble-topped stand before us. "There now, tea, sugar, lemon, cream, cookies—that should take of everything. Chloe will serve you, Mr. Sawyer."

He smiled up at my mother. "That's Em, Mrs. Spencer. Call me Em."

"Yes, of course."

I looked first at Mr. Sawyer, then at my mother. He had to be more than ten years older than she. She must have read my mind, for, after throwing me a warning glare, she fluttered from the room.

I decided that Mr. Sawyer might be uncomfortable in a lady's drawing room, but I would give him no cause to censure my manners. I served the tea with the flair of a duchess. "Sugar? Cream?" The muscles in my cheeks ached from forcing a smile. "How about one of Ma's sugar cookies?"

We sipped our tea to the tick of my grandmother's mantel clock. "So, Mr. Sawyer, er, Em, tell me about yourself and about your son Charley."

While I appeared to be listening to his life history, I eyed the hands of the clock. Once or twice they moved so slowly I was certain the heirloom needed winding. The clock gonged at the half-hour. Feeling the urge to yawn, I covered my mouth with my hand.

"Excuse me. It's been a long day, washday, you know."

Catching my hint, he rose to his feet. "I would like to see you again, Miss Chloe—perhaps, tomorrow evening?"

I batted my eyes and simpered, "I'm not sure about tomorrow. Perhaps later in the week." *What am I doing? This isn't me!*

"Uh, oh, yes. There's a grange meeting Thursday evening. I'd be honored if you would allow me to escort you."

I gulped. *Be seen with him in public?* All hopes of keeping this courtship business secret evaporated. Somehow I'd backed myself into a corner. "Yes, that would be fine."

He took my arm and led me to the hallway. "I'll call for you at seven."

"Fine. I'll be ready."

I hated my duplicity. I wanted to tell him outright that he was wasting his time, that he should look for a woman nearer his own age, for I would never agree to marry him.

No one spoke when I returned to the kitchen. The younger children had already gone to bed. Joe had left for town. Ma sat in the rocker by the fire, knitting. Pa sat at the table reading a Pittsburgh newspaper. Hattie sat across from him darning the boys' stockings. They all avoided my gaze. I squared my shoulders and marched up the stairs to my room. If they wanted a martyr, I'd give them a martyr.

Later, when Hattie tiptoed into our room, I pretended to be asleep. Downstairs I heard Pa drop the heavy oak bar into place across the kitchen door, then bolt the front door. I closed my eyes, certain I wouldn't be able to sleep at all.

Pounding on the kitchen door awakened me. I listened to the floorboards creak as someone crossed the kitchen toward the door, then the sound of the heavy oakbar being lifted from its metal brace.

I blinked and rubbed my eyes, wondering how long I'd been asleep. I'd been dreaming of mice, the little dark brown ones that hid in the loft and in the cornfields behind the railway station. In my dream, the usually timid creatures formed a battleline between me and the ticket office. Their black beads of eyes stared menacingly, alert to my slightest movement, daring me to approach. One of them had begun creeping forward, when Pa coughed, causing the mice to scurry back between the cornstalks.

I heard the urgent whispering of male voices—my father's and Franklin's. I knew Myrtle's first baby was due any time during the next few weeks. "Not tonight. Please, not tonight," I groaned.

No matter how much I argued with myself, I knew the truth. So, sighing, I hugged myself and counted, "One, two, three, four—"

The light from a kerosene lantern at the foot of the stairs danced up the stairwell. "Chloe, wake up. Myrtle's gone into labor."

I continued counting. "Five, six, seven, eight—"

Pa called louder this time, "Chloe? Are you awake? Myrtle needs you."

"Nine . . . ten." I stretched out the ten as long as possible, reluctant to leave the warm hollow I'd made under the woolen quilts. *Why do babies decide to be born at such inconvenient times?* I remembered Auntie Gert's words, "First babies are always the hardest." I shivered and slid my feet out onto the bare hardwood floor.

Behind me, Ori stirred and mumbled, "Is it morning yet?"

I tucked the covers tightly about Ori. "No, little one. Go back to sleep." Ma was up; I could hear her ease back the ash pan on the cookstove to allow air to fan up through the burners. The thud of the first log being stuffed into the stove sounded.

My father coughed again, a long, rattling wheeze. "Chloe? I'm goin' to hitch up the team. You hurry down now, ya' hear?"

"Yes, Pa." I stumbled over to the ceramic wash basin and lifted the pitcher of water. A thin sheet of ice had formed on the water during the night. I broke the ice with my hairbrush, then poured the water into the basin. Shivering, I splashed the cold water on my face, toweled my numb skin, and reached for my linsey-woolsey dress hanging on the third nail to the right of the night stand. As I finished buckling my shoes, I heard Ma's teakettle whistling.

I glanced longingly at my sleeping sisters, then tiptoed out of the room and down the stairs. As I passed the window on the landing, I scraped a fingernail across one of the panes. *There's ice on the inside of the window. Must be a heavy frost out there.*

Ma placed a second kerosene lamp on the table, bathing the room in a warm, golden light. Pa's leather medicine case sat at the end of the long oak table. "No need to tell me, girl. This is the coldest May I can remember. Your dad's cough is worse because of it."

I hurried to the cookstove and made myself a cup of hot peppermint tea. I cozied the hot mug between my hands. "Think we'll lose the corn?"

"Could be . . ." Ma shrugged and idly massaged her

abdomen. "Tell Myrtle I wanted to be there with her, but Pa says this young-un needs my attention right now." Her voice trailed off into a sigh.

I placed a hand on my mother's shoulder. "Ma, are you feeling all right?"

At the sound of horses and wagon pulling up outside, she brushed my hand aside. "Now, bundle up, you hear? Don't want you comin' down with consumption. And don't forget your father's bag."

I studied my mother's face for a moment. Worry and exhaustion had whittled away her energy, leaving her too hollow eyed and harsh looking for a woman in her midthirties.

I slipped into my wool hand-me-down coat and wrapped my red shawl around my neck. "I'll be fine, Ma, really." I picked up the case and headed toward the door. As I opened the door, a gust of frigid wind snatched my breath away. I gasped and ran for the buckboard.

My father reached down and hauled me up next to him on the seat. "How far along did Franklin say she is?"

"He had no idea whatsoever." I adjusted my knitted scarf over my nose and snuggled close to Pa. It felt good to talk as equals once again. I sensed that he felt the same way.

"Giddyap!" Pa clicked his tongue and flicked the reins. Steam billowed from the horses' nostrils as the wagon lurched forward.

"This sudden cold snap is gonna' damage the fruit trees and, probably, a whole lot more." The reins dangled between his fingers as he blew on his hands. "How are you feeling this morning?"

I shrugged. "As well as can be expected."

He opened his mouth to speak, then clamped it shut. We rode in silence for what seemed like forever. Finally he spoke. "Wonder what's happening between the United States and Spain in the Philippines now."

"No idea." I glanced over at the newly planted fields, white with a heavy layer of frost. I hated the awkward barrier erected between us, yet I felt pleased knowing that he hated it too.

"Riley's thinking seriously about enlisting."

The mention of my eldest brother forced me to communicate. I shook my head in disgust. "I don't understand why a bunch of rabble-rousing sailors on the other side of the earth should influence my big brother to enlist."

Pa chuckled. "Men are like that, I'm afraid. Women have babies, and men fight wars—kind of keeps things balanced."

I stared at the road ahead and thought about my father's words. In the distance, I could see the town's cluster of roofs. The clop of the horses' hooves echoed as we crossed the bridge over Honeyoye Creek at the edge of town.

"Is Emmett coming by tonight?" Pa waited for a response.

"No. Thursday night." I avoided his gaze by staring at the row of darkened houses along Main Street, envious of the inhabitants burrowed beneath their quilts. The same was not true at Myrtle and Franklin's clapboard cottage. Light shone from every window.

Ashen-faced, Franklin met us at the door. "You're finally here!" While Pa cared for the team, I followed my brother-in-law into the house. A wave of warmth accosted me as I crossed the threshold.

"When did Myrtle go into labor?" I asked as I handed him my coat and shawl.

"Oh . . ." Franklin frowned and stroked his chin, as if I'd asked him to tabulate the national budget or recite the United States Constitution by heart. "She complained of a backache last night at the supper table." He pointed up the flight of stairs. "She's up there." The wail I heard from the room over my head made his directions superfluous. I hoisted my skirts around my ankles and bounded up to their room.

He tagged after me like a chicken at feeding time. "What can I do to help?"

During my short experience as a midwife, I had quickly discovered that a nervous husband must be kept busy, or he'd drive both me and his wife to distraction. "Boil water—lots of water. And I'll call you when I need you."

The moment I stuck my head around the doorjamb, Myrtle burst into tears. "Oh, Chloe Mae, I'm so glad you finally got here. Where's Ma? I need Ma."

I hurried to my sister. "She wanted to come, but she's feeling poorly this morning. Pa thought it best she stay home." I held Myrtle's hand and gleaned as much information from her as I could until her next contraction arrived. After examining the baby's progress, I realized we were in for a long night.

By dawn, the baby still hadn't appeared. Pa sat with Myrtle while I cooked a batch of oatmeal for the three of us and boiled a pot of herb tea for the mother-to-be. Franklin drove all of us crazy by pacing to the bedroom door and back. Finally, in exasperation, I suggested, "Go sell some tickets or something. I'll come and get you when the baby arrives." Franklin was the ticket agent at the railway station.

Pa and I worked side by side, cleaning up the kitchen. It was a strange experience. I couldn't remember a time when my father had dried a dish or washed the tabletop. When we returned upstairs, we found Myrtle asleep. I straightened her blankets and tiptoed from the room.

"The tea relaxed her, Pa. You might as well go to work. That baby's taking his own sweet time coming, I'm afraid." Pa nodded and gave my hand a squeeze.

His apologetic smile brought tears to my eyes. I watched him lumber down the stairs and listened as he shrugged into his overcoat. Then the front door slammed behind him. I glanced about the room. Because everything was ready for the birth, there was nothing much for me to do but catch a short nap until Myrtle needed me.

Myrtle and Franklin's first son, Franklin Joseph, arrived late that afternoon. Once I had the exhausted mother and irate infant clean and comfortable, I told my sister I would go get her husband. She smiled sleepily, nodded, and caressed her son's downy dark brown hair.

I ran down the stairs, slipped into my coat, and hurried out of the house. It felt good to get out of the stuffy house for a while. The chill predawn temperatures had given way to a warm, sunny day. It was as if the day itself was celebrating the birth of my nephew. Joy bubbled up inside me as I skipped down the street toward the train station. One block over, and I was running between the train track and a recently planted cornfield. I remembered my interrupted dream and laughed. *Not a mouse in sight!*

I paused beside the track to watch a freight train pull out of the station. Visions of faraway places with magical names like New York, Pittsburgh, and Chicago cavorted through my imagination. When I was a little girl, Pa often brought the family to town to watch the trains coming and going from the station. I'd wave at well-dressed men and women sitting inside the passenger cars and wish I could go wherever the train was going. *Someday, maybe,* I told myself. *Someday . . .*

As the train reached the edge of the platform, a young man darted out of the cornfield and scrambled on board. I held my breath until his feet disappeared inside the boxcar.

After watching until the train rounded the bend of the river, I hurried toward the depot. Franklin must have seen me coming, for we collided at the first set of double doors leading into the building.

"Tell me—is she—is the baby—"

I laughed and slipped my arm in his. "Myrtle's just fine. Come on, let's go home and meet your son."

"My son? I've got a son?" He whirled around and shouted to a waiting room of startled passengers. "I've got a son!"

Smiles broke out as well as a hearty applause. Not waiting for further congratulations, Franklin bolted out the door and down the street toward home. I did my best to keep up, but my skirt slowed my progress. I rounded the corner in time to see my brother Joe pull up in front of Myrtle and Franklin's place in Pa's wagon.

"Hi," I called. "Heard the news? It's a boy." I hurried to his side. "What are you doing here?"

He took my arm and led me into the house. "Pa sent me. Ma slipped on the porch this morning when she went out to feed the chickens."

I stopped. "The baby?"

Joe shrugged. "He's not sure."

We stepped into the hallway. I whispered to my brother, "You go up and see the baby while I gather my things. Don't say anything about Ma yet. There's time enough for that later."

I examined Myrtle and little Franklin once more before heading home. "Stay in bed and get lots of rest. I'll be back tomorrow morning to be sure you and the baby are faring well."

Myrtle grasped my hand in hers. "Thank you, Chloe Mae."

After kissing her cheek, I reached across the bed and caressed my new nephew's tiny hand. "Take good care of this little guy." I stood up and walked to the bedroom door. "Hattie will come in with me tomorrow. She'll probably want to stay and help you for a few days."

Myrtle smiled wearily. "That would be nice."

"See you tomorrow." I waved goodbye to my sister and threw a kiss to the sleeping baby.

After leaving strict instructions with Franklin to let his wife get as much sleep as possible, I hurried to the wagon. Joe took the medicine bag from my hands and helped me climb aboard. I'd barely adjusted my skirt when my brother flicked the reins. The wagon lurched forward. I hit the wagon bench with a thud. He darted a concerned glance my way. "Sorry. You're all right, aren't you?"

I grabbed for a handrail and for the back of the bench. "No thanks to you."

He flicked the reins again. "Sorry, I guess I'm a little distracted. Something came up today . . ."

Surprised, I waited for him to continue. Joe was never one to reveal his feelings to others. When he remained silent for longer than I thought necessary, I scowled at him. "Aren't you going to tell me about it?"

He ruminated for a moment while my fingers tapped out my impatience on my lap. When he finally spoke, each of his words seemed wrenched from him. "Mr. Chamberlain sent for me today. He's sending Cy to San Francisco, and he wants me to go along as a baby sitter."

"A baby sitter? How does Cy feel about this?"

My brother shrugged. "Cy will think I'm along as a

groom for his thoroughbred Morgans while I'm really being paid to report Cy's shenanigans to Mr. Chamberlain."

"So, when do you leave?"

"Leave? Who says I'm going to take the job?"

"What? Pass up a chance to go to California? That's halfway to China. Well, maybe not quite halfway . . ."

Joe waved his finger in my face. "The idea of spying on Cy repulses me."

"I don't believe you. You are crazy!" My lip curled in disgust. "All the man wants you to do is keep tabs on his son? If it were me, I'd spy on the queen of England in order to go to California!"

That's when I first realized nature had played a cruel trick on Joe and me. Our personalities should have been reversed. Nothing would make my brother happier than to settle down in Osweo Valley and raise a herd of horses and a passel of kids. But me—I ached to see the world I'd read about for so many years—see it all for myself.

Joe's shoulders slumped. "There's more. Besides covering all my expenses, Cy's old man's offered to set me up in my own livery after three years."

I grabbed his arm and shrieked, "I don't believe it. Your very own livery? When do you leave?"

He laughed in spite of himself. "I haven't agreed to go—"

"But you will!"

"I don't know."

One of the wagon wheels hit a rut in the road. "What did Pa say when you told him?"

Joe brought the team to a stop in front of the house. "I haven't told him yet, what with him worried about Ma and all."

"Oh well, you know what he'll say."

Joe nodded. "He'll tell me to jump at the chance."

He looked so woebegone that I reached out and squeezed his hand. "I'd better go inside and see if Ma needs me. Hey, you do what's best for you, all right?"

Taking the porch steps two at a time, I burst into the house. "How's Ma?"

Hattie sat in Ma's rocker, reading Pa's Bible—I noticed she did that a lot since her accident. She put her finger to her lips. "She's sleeping right now. Pa thinks she'll be just fine. How are Myrtle and the baby?"

"They're doing great. She looks forward to seeing you tomorrow." I set the medicine bag behind the door and removed my coat and scarf. My little sister Ori bounded down the stairs and into my arms. I squeezed her, then asked, "Hey, Precious, what have you been up to?"

Ori's smile faded into a frown. "Ma's sick. I've been taking care of Dorothy all day long. The boys are helping Pa with the evening chores."

I gave the little girl a kiss on the cheek and put her down. "You are such a sweetheart. What would Hattie do without you?"

My little sister's eyes brightened. She leaned close as if to confide a secret. "And the baby?"

I tickled her under the chin. "It's a boy."

Ori groaned. "Oh no, another Worley!"

"Or, perhaps, another Jesse." I knew Orinda idolized her nine-year-old brother, Jesse, the seventh in the Spencer clan.

Hattie struggled out of the rocking chair and winced. Massaging her lame thigh, she limped over to the stove. "You'd better not leave Dorothy alone too long, Ori. She might get hurt."

"All right." I watched Ori bound back upstairs.

She has to be the most even-tempered one in this family. Exhausted, I stretched, then dropped into my customary place at the table. "So tell me, what happened here?"

Hattie lifted the cover from a casserole dish. The aroma of potatoes au gratin caused my stomach to growl. "M-m-m, I didn't realize how hungry I was. That oatmeal this morning didn't stick long enough."

My sister placed a clean plate on the table before me and handed me a fork. "You eat while I tell you all about it."

I finished my meal and leaned back and groaned. The events of the long day washed over me. I considered telling my sister about Joe's offer, then changed my mind—it wasn't my story to tell. All I could think of was heading upstairs to bed. Then I remembered Ma. "I should look in on Ma."

Hattie nodded. When I opened the door to my parents' room and peeked in, I found my mother sleeping peacefully and decided not to wake her. As I closed the bedroom door, I felt a tender hand on my shoulder.

"Go to bed, Chloe." Hattie's eyes were filled with compassion. "Anyone can see that you're dead on your feet. Ori and I can handle supper cleanup tonight."

"But I can't leave you—"

She tucked a stray curl behind my right ear. "You can and you will. Besides, Ma may not be out of danger. So get some sleep while you can."

"You are so good to me. Have I ever told you how much I love you?" Hattie's eyes misted over as I kissed her blushing cheek. My throat knotted with emotion. Hattie was the family's steadying force, the person everyone took for granted—me, Pa, Ma, my brothers and sisters, all of us. She cooked our meals, helped my mother with the younger children, and washed and mended our clothing without a word of complaint. Why hadn't I noticed it before? I searched her face for a trace of resentment, but found none.

The sound of Pa and the boys returning from evening chores broke the moment. Hattie cleared her throat and hurried to the sideboard for the necessary tableware. "Send the girls down for their supper."

Ori and Dorothy met me at the landing. I kissed them good night and stumbled into the bedroom. As I unbuttoned my dress, the everyday sounds of life drifted up from the kitchen below. I could hear Amby and Jesse arguing about whose turn it was to haul wood while Pa scolded Worley for snatching the heel of bread before the blessing. A wave of loneliness hit me. So much was changing: Riley enlisting; Myrtle married with a new baby; Joe leaving for California; and—if my parents had their way—I'd be marrying Emmett Sawyer. Of all of us, only Hattie seemed permanent.

After several days the threat of a miscarriage passed, and Ma could leave her bed. She appeared the same on the outside, but inside, she had changed. While she hadn't lost the baby, she had lost her ability to laugh. Without the laughter, her Irish spirit turned bitter; her sarcasm indiscriminately sliced through people's feelings liked a surgeon's scalpel.

We all felt her ire. Pa spent more time with patients. After accepting Mr. Chamberlain's offer, Joe stayed at the stables evenings and weekends, getting the horses and the necessary supplies ready for the journey west. The younger boys stayed outside the house as long as possible each day. I watched helplessly as Ori and Dorothy came downstairs reluctantly, while I escaped to my books. This left poor Hattie to face Ma's foul moods alone, with nowhere to hide. The only reprieve occurred when Emmett showed up at the house; then Ma polished her company silver and her company manners.

Fourth of July Fireworks

Emmett's ardor increased in direct proportion to my distaste. Each time I dressed for his arrival, I vowed to give the man a fair chance. And each time he left our home, I vowed I'd never put myself through such torture again. I think what I hated most was hearing about his grudge matches. He told and retold the details of everyone he bested since his grade-school days.

"I really told him a thing or two. If he thought he could treat me like that, well, he had another think coming!" As Emmett boasted of his exploits, I visualized a Plymouth Rock rooster, strutting about the hen yard, challenging every bush and rock. When I tried to change the subject, I soon learned there were no safe subjects. For a man who, on our first date, said he had no opinions, Emmett Sawyer had opinions on everything. He had no time for religion—"all preachers are scoundrels." His opinions on current events sounded vaguely similar to his personal altercations with people. "If I were in the U.S. Cavalry, I'd show them Injuns a thing or two. If I were the president, I'd blast the daylights out of those Spaniards. If I were married to a suffragette, I'd teach her to toe the line. If I ... If I ... If I ...!"

His "If I's" were not the worst of it. After our first three or four evenings alone in the parlor, Emmett's

75

fears about someone walking in on us relaxed. And so began our game of "thrust and parry" the entire length of the sofa. First his arm would be on the back of the sofa; a few seconds later, his hand would be caressing my neck. I'd inch away. Or he'd capture my hand on my lap, and his fingers would begin drawing spirals on my knee. I'd try to distract him by offering to pour him another cup of Ma's herbal tea.

At the end of each date, I'd stagger from his presence in search of a sympathetic ear, usually Hattie's. I'd find her sitting in the kitchen, reading the family Bible or mending the boys' socks. I'd storm into the room and throw myself down in a side chair.

"The man's an ape. Hauling on his boots in the morning uses up two-thirds of his available brain power for the day!" Hattie would just smile that calm little smile of hers. Feeling suddenly guilty for not being grateful that a man, any man, would find me attractive, I'd swallow the rest of my complaints.

When Joe came home to spend a few weeks with us before leaving for California, I dogged his footsteps. Not only did I need a friendly ear, but I hungered for every detail about the upcoming trip.

One evening toward the end of June, Riley, Myrtle, her husband, and baby joined us for a special supper. While Joe wouldn't be leaving for at least another week, it was his evening, and everyone, even Ma, seemed determined to make it truly special for him. My quiet, unassuming brother held us all spellbound as he described his upcoming adventure.

"Mr. Chamberlain has arranged for Cy and me to travel to California in the company's Pullman car. We'll have our very own butler and cook. If he had to rent the car, it would cost him fifty dollars a day. Imagine fifty dollars a day!"

Amby gasped in awe. "It will be like traveling across the country in the comfort of Ma's parlor."

Joe ruffled his younger brother's hair. "Better. We each will have our own bedroom. There's even a built-in bathtub and all the hot water we could want."

Pa shook his head. "What a change from our trip west from Delaware, hmm, Annie?"

Tears glistened in Ma's eyes as she gazed the length of the table at Pa. "A farm wagon, covered with canvas, two of my da's farm horses, and a small collection of household goods."

Ori tipped her head to one side. "But Ma, how did you have room for Grandma Lewis's breakfront?"

Ma smiled. "That came later by rail—after Da died."

Worley tugged at Ma's sleeve. "Why didn't you take the train from Delaware? Didn't you have trains then?"

Pa laughed. "We had trains, but not much money—at least, not enough to get us to Potter County. But we had a treasure chest of dreams, son. So, go on, Joe—tell us more."

"Well, I'll be caring for Chamberlain's two Morgans. They'll have their own stock car specially outfitted—"

Worley interrupted. "With their own bathtub?"

"No, not quite, but just about everything else you can imagine. They'll travel better than most of the other passengers on the train. They'll have all the oats they can eat and water they can drink and private quarters to do it in."

"Wow!" I watched Worley's eyes fill with admiration. "I wish I could go too. I'd be happy just to ride with the horses."

Me too, I grumbled to myself.

"If all goes well, we'll be in San Francisco in less than a week. Do you realize that we'll be traveling at speeds up to sixty miles per hour?"

Again Pa shook his head in amazement. "Next thing you know, they'll perfect this airplane contraption and make the steam engine obsolete."

"Humph!" Ma grunted. "If God intended people to fly, He'd have given them wings!"

Pa chuckled and winked at my mother. "Stranger things have happened, my sweet."

Everyone laughed at our parents' exchange; we'd heard it so many times before. It felt good to hear Ma and Pa banter once again. It had been so long.

Joe nodded toward Riley. "What about you? By the looks of things, you might be leaving Pennsylvania too."

Riley's eyes sparkled with the very mention of war. "You can be sure of that, little brother. The minute President McKinley gives the word, my boss will have seen the last of me."

I glanced toward my father. His eyes saddened at the mention of war. He was a man of conflicting emotions—both a man of action and a man of peace. "Even though I was a little boy when Fort Sumter fell to the Confederates, I remember the day Dad and my two older brothers signed up with the Union army, while my dad's cousin, Horton, enlisted in the army of the Confederacy.

"In a border state like Delaware, the war divided a lot of our neighbors' families." Pa stared down at his hands for several moments before continuing. "I can also remember when my parents, my sister, and I traveled east by rail to Gettysburg for the dedication of the battlefield. As I stared out over that quiet field, I realized for the first time that my big brother would never come home again. He died defending issues I couldn't understand."

My mouth dropped open in surprise. "Pa, I never knew you actually heard President Lincoln's famous speech."

Jesse whistled through his teeth. "Wow! We had to learn that whole speech in history class this year."

Pa chuckled. "Be glad you didn't have to learn Edward Everett's speech; he spoke for more than two hours." While the rest of us laughed at Jesse's horror, my father sobered. "Our family is changing so rapidly. Myrtle and Franklin have established a new home and have produced my first grandson. Riley might be heading south to Cuba or west to the Philippines. Joe, you'll be in California. And by the looks of things . . ." He grinned with pleasure at me. ". . . wedding bells will soon be ringing for Chloe Mae. God has been good to us."

At the mention of wedding bells, my smile faded. I stared down at my lap. How long could I allow this farce of a courtship with Emmett to continue? Was I being fair, not telling the man the truth? It's not that I hadn't tried. But like it or not, I had no intention of becoming his second wife or the mother of his fourteen-year-old son and of the long succession of sons he planned to sire.

That night, after the rest of the family retired for the night, I sneaked out of the house. For a while I sat on the porch railing, listening to the chirping of crickets. Patches sidled up to my ankles, demanding attention. As I reached down to pet him, I heard a train whistle and thought of Joe, upstairs sleeping in the boys' room once again.

The dog and I ambled down the steps and across the yard. In a moment of whimsy, I stretched my arms upward as if to capture one of heaven's glittering bodies. I sighed. The stars I could see and a God I couldn't see both remained tantalizingly out of reach. This wasn't the first night since Emmett had invaded my comfortable little world that I'd slipped out of the house to do battle with my father's God.

As I rounded the south corner of the barn, I noticed a

light shining in the loft. Curious, I entered the barn and climbed the ladder.

"Is that you, Chloe Mae?" My father's face peered over the end of the ladder.

"Pa? What are you doing out here at this hour? I thought you went to bed."

"I did, but I couldn't sleep." He reached down and helped me up the last rung.

"Me either."

An array of gold coins spread out on Pa's worktable captured my attention. "Pa, where did you get all that money?"

"Da, Grandpa Lewis, left them to you kids, his grandchildren. Twenty-dollar gold pieces—one for each of you upon reaching adulthood. I keep them right here in the bottom of Ma's trunk." He wrapped his arm about my shoulders and led me over to the table. "I was just choosing Joe's. Riley and Myrtle already have theirs."

The coins sparkled in the mellow lantern light. I picked up one and examined it. I'd never held anything so beautiful in my hands—the coin outshone any star I'd tried to catch.

Pa placed his hands on my shoulders. "And when you marry Emmett, I'll give you yours."

I swallowed hard. "And if I don't marry Emmett?"

"Oh, Chloe, when will you stop being foolish? Of course you'll marry Emmett."

Gently, I shook my head and replaced the coin beside the others. I whirled about and buried my face in my father's broad chest. He tightened his arms about me. I'd missed him so much since Ma's illness. I wanted to tell him of the very real war inside me. But I couldn't risk ruining these precious moments we had together.

"Oh, Pa, I love you so much. Never ever forget that, no matter what I do."

"You are my lovely daughter, a jewel in my earthly crown." He patted my head and shoulders gently. "What could you ever do to disappoint me?"

Instinctively, I squeezed him tighter, afraid to speak.

On July first, the United States army had taken Havana's San Juan Hill. On July third the Spanish fleet was in full rout. And on July fourth, I declared full-out war on Emmett Sawyer. I would tell him the truth—that I didn't love him, and never could. Though I realized that the annual Fourth of July celebration was not an ideal time to tell him, I knew the right time would come, and it would come soon.

Emmett was escorting me to the holiday parade and town picnic. When I invited him and his son to eat with my family, he suggested I pack a separate picnic lunch for just the two of us. Reluctantly, I agreed. On the morning of the Fourth, my mother met me at the foot of the stairs. In her hands she held a yellow cambric dress. "Here, Chloe Mae, for you."

I couldn't believe my eyes. "Ma, it's the prettiest gown I've ever seen."

She beamed with pride as I ran my hands gently over the lace along the upper bodice and neck. From the moment I slipped it on, I loved it. I ran to the hall mirror and gasped with pleasure at my reflection.

Ma followed me. She clapped her hands with delight, then set to buttoning the long row of buttons up the back. Her face shone with happiness as she wrapped a three-inch wide, rust-colored satin ribbon about my waist, tying a perfect bow. The ends of the bow dangled halfway down the back of my skirt.

"It's beautiful, Ma. It's just like a dress in the catalog." I whirled about to face her. "Thank you so much. But how did you make it without my knowing?"

"Hattie modeled it for me." She flushed and puffed the sleeves into shape. "Every girl needs one pretty dress to remember."

Swooshing about in front of the mirror, I tore off my nightcap. My fiery curls tumbled down about my shoulders. That's when I decided not to braid my hair. Borrowing a set of Ma's ivory combs, I caught up the front and sides of my hair into a scrap of satin ribbon Ma had left over. I would carry the matching bonnet instead of wearing it. As I wrapped a loose tendril about my finger, then patted it into place at the side of my face, I thought of Hattie and frowned. Poor Hattie. Surely she would have enjoyed a new dress also. I reminded myself to thank her later.

Emmett arrived at the house an hour before the morning parade was scheduled to begin. I met him at the door with basket in hand. When he saw me, he uttered a low, appreciative whistle.

"Chloe Mae, you sure are a purty little thing." He took the basket from my hands, placed my arm in his, and led me to his wagon. After helping me into the wagon, he sat down beside me. As he flicked the reins with his right hand, he ran the fingers of his left hand over the back of my neck and whispered in my ear, "Almost as purty as you were that day splashing in the creek."

How could he mention that afternoon! My face suffused with color. I stared straight ahead, refusing to meet his gaze. He snarled at my coolness. "Boy, you sure have turned out to be a real prude."

The sound of a surrey coming up beside us broke the tension. Emmett edged his team over to the right to allow the Webster family to pass. Mrs. Webster waved. "Hey, you two lovebirds, you're going to be late for the parade if you don't hurry."

I smiled and waved back. "See you there."

Emmett and I didn't speak for the rest of the trip to town. Throughout the morning's parade, he remained granite silent. His son, Charley, who had ridden to town with some friends, came up to say Hi. When he saw his father's dour expression, the boy shot a frightened glance my way, then excused himself and melted into the crowd.

The local regiment of Civil War veterans marched past, followed by a brigade of shiny new bicycles. Stan Kirkpatrick and his very pregnant wife Sally joined us. Immediately, Sally started chatting about the sewing room she'd made over for the baby. Stan tried to strike up a conversation with Emmett, but he ignored the younger man.

"Are you two going to the picnic?" Sally's face glowed with happiness. "You could eat with us if you'd like."

I glanced toward Emmett, then back at Sally. "I appreciate your invitation, but Emmett has planned a special—"

"Say no more." Sally giggled. "I remember our courtin' days."

Stan grinned down at his blushing wife. "You should; it was less than two years ago."

The volunteer fire brigade marched past, signaling the end of the parade. Emmett mumbled something about getting the lunch basket. Sensing his foul mood, Sally and Stan said their goodbyes and joined the spectators making their way to the Veterans' Park for lunch. Wanting to savor my short reprieve from Emmett, I walked slowly, allowing the jostling crowd to pass me by. Children and dogs scooted in and around my skirt, but I barely noticed. Suddenly I felt a hand on my elbow. I sighed and closed my eyes. *How did he return so fast with the basket?*

"Well, hello again, Miss Chloe."

My mouth dropped open as I glanced over my left shoulder into the face of Phillip Chamberlain. "Phillip, what a surprise."

Pleasure at seeing him again wreathed my face with delight until I looked past Phillip's smiling face into Emmett's furious one. His eyes snapped with anger. He reached around Phillip and grasped me by my other elbow. "Chloe Mae, I have reserved us a spot down by the walking bridge. If you'll excuse us, Mr. Chamberlain."

Emmett made the name Chamberlain sound like a distasteful disease. Phillip's eyebrows shot up as he studied my face for a reaction. My face reddened. How I wished I had the courage to refuse to go with Emmett. Instead, I gazed down at the roadway. Phillip tipped his hat to me. "Miss Spencer, it's been lovely seeing you again. Mr. Sawyer."

"Mr. Chamberlain," Emmett mumbled under his breath as he whirled me about and directed me up the road toward the park. His grip on my elbow hurt. Neighbors nodded and greeted us as they passed.

"Emmett," I hissed through my best "company" smile, "you're hurting me. Please let go." I couldn't make a scene.

"Hurting! Someone needs to take you in hand, woman."

I struggled to keep pace with his long, angry stride. When we reached the park, he led me away from the congregating picnickers to a secluded spot between a row of forsythia bushes and the riverbank. By the time we reached the basket and Ma's quilt, I'd been dragged as far as I intended to be dragged. I yanked my arm free and clenched my fists for battle.

"Emmett Sawyer! Don't you ever handle me like that again!"

The fire exploding behind his eyes shot fear through me. I sensed that he was going to hit me. Instead, he wrapped his arms about me, pinning my hands at my sides. He pressed himself against me until it felt like I couldn't breathe. I struggled to no avail. I tried to kick him in the shins, but my skirt hampered my movement.

"If you don't let me go this instant, I'll scream."

He must have believed me, for he suddenly released me. Uninvited tears of anger welled up in my eyes. I clenched my fists and ground my teeth in frustration as a slow smirk formed at the corners of his mouth.

"You are a feisty little morsel, aren't you? Don't worry, I can bide my time." He leaned against the tree trunk and narrowed his eyes. "I'll enjoy taming you."

"I beg your pardon?" My right heel danced to the beat of Indian war drums.

He opened his eyes and smirked. "I know how to tame a woman. You'll settle down once I get my hands on you. Just ask my first wife—if you could."

I gulped down a massive lump of anger in my throat. *Calm down, Chloe. Now's the time to tell him how you feel.*

Stepping beyond his reach, I muttered, "Not this woman." Before he could respond, I whipped about and faced him. "Emmett, I had planned to say this graciously, but after your ungentlemanly behavior today, I see no need to be subtle." I clasped and unclasped my hands behind me. "I do not love you, and I never will love you because I do not respect you. I will explain to my father—"

He sneered. "Your father! He spoiled you rotten, lettin' you think you're as smart as a man. Now, it's up to me to turn you into an obedient wife."

I sighed. "I've said all I have to say, Emmett. If you'll excuse me now, I would like to join my family." I reached down to pick up the basket, when his hand shot out, trapping my wrist in an iron vice. Choking back a new flood of tears, I refused to give him the satisfaction of knowing how much he was hurting me. He pushed me down on the quilt and growled through clenched teeth.

"You will rejoin your family when I say so. Is that clear? And if anyone hears so much as a whimper from you, I will make sure no man who values his good name will ever look at you seriously again, is that clear? Small town gossips can be so cruel." He relaxed his grip and blew a loose tendril away from my ear. "Also, I will determine the length of this courtship, not you."

I wrenched free, nursing my bruised wrist with my other hand. Emmett leaned back against the tree trunk and ran his fingers through the cascade of curls down my back. "Serve my meal, Chloe."

At any moment, I expected him to grab my hair and pull me to him. He didn't. Instead, he ran his fingers lightly up and down my back. "By the way, I've been thinking an August wedding would be appropriate. We'll announce our engagement to your parents tonight after the fireworks."

Announce our engagement? An August wedding? You can't do this to me, you can't! Woodenly, I opened the basket and removed the bowls of potato salad, baked beans, and carrot sticks. My breath came in short, ragged gasps as if I'd been crying for hours. I dished out a serving of potato salad, fearing what might happen if the other picnickers left for the afternoon games at the schoolhouse. Beads of cold sweat broke out on my forehead, and I fought off the urge to faint.

Now is not the time to panic. First I need to get away from him, I thought. *Later I can handle the rest of the problem.* As I sliced the strawberry pie into individual servings, I prayed for an escape. Seconds later I heard my brother Amby calling my name.

I leaped to my feet before Emmett could restrain me and ran to the edge of the forsythia hedge. "Over here, Amby. Over here by the riverbank."

My brother pushed through the hedge. "Pa sent me to find you. I've been looking all over." He leaned down, his hands on his knees, as he struggled to catch his breath. "Sally Kirkpatrick twisted her ankle and fell. She's gone into labor. Pa says come right away."

"I'll run on ahead, Amby, while you stay here and help Emmett gather up Ma's dishes."

"Don't forget what I said," Emmett called. "Tonight we tell your folks."

Without looking back, I gathered up my skirt in both hands and bolted through the bushes to the roadway. Pa saw me running toward him and drove the team to meet me. He reached down and grabbed my bruised wrist to help me into the wagon. I winced, but he failed to notice.

He hauled me into the seat beside him and flicked the reins. "Sally took quite a tumble. Stan took her home a few minutes ago. The labor came on instantly."

Fortunately, the Kirkpatricks lived on the same side of town as the park. When we arrived, I hopped down from the wagon and ran inside the house. My father followed me. I hurried to Sally while Pa convinced Stan to drive him home for his medicine bag.

The men returned with the bag, and I brewed a pot of Pa's special tea for Sally. A few minutes after drinking her second cup, she began to relax, and the frequency of her contractions decreased. Suggesting the men leave the room and let her rest, I closed the door behind them and made myself comfortable in the rocker by the bedroom window.

Long, golden shafts of light tinted the little bedroom.

I smiled to myself. *If Emmett plans to announce our engagement tonight, he can very well do it alone!* I sent a grateful smile at my patient. Unaware of my thoughts, Sally smiled back, stretched, then closed her eyes. The steady creak of the rocking chair lulled both of us to sleep.

I awoke hours later to a dusky blue twilight. I glanced down at the afghan someone had thrown over me. Disorientated, I gazed about the room. *Sally!* I thought. *Sally Kirkpatrick!* I started from the chair.

"Hi, Chloe." Sally smiled from her pillow.

"Oh, Sally, I'm so sorry I fell asleep."

"That's all right. I'm doing fine. I haven't had a contraction since I drank your father's herb tea." She smiled and sighed. "Speaking of your Pa, he said to tell you he went back to the park and would send Emmett for you after the fireworks."

Emmett! Alarms jangled in my mind; my stomach lurched. I grabbed for one of the finials on Sally's mahogany bedstead. *There is no possible way I would consider riding home alone with him.* I didn't even want to see him again, ever again. My face must have revealed my thoughts.

Sally eyed me curiously. "Is something wrong? Are you feeling all right?"

I took a deep breath. "Just a moment of dizziness. Probably jumped up too fast. Would you drink another cup of tea if I fixed it for you?"

She rolled her eyes toward the ceiling. "More tea? I could eat a team of horses about now. I never did get a taste of my mother's cherry cobbler today."

I shrugged. "It might be wise not to put too much food in your stomach right now until we're sure everything's back to normal."

"Oh, all right. A cup of tea it is. May I have some

clover tea instead of the bitter stuff your father made?"

"I'll see what I can find." I left the bedroom and descended the stairs to the kitchen, where I found Stan hunched over a plate of cold baked beans.

He sprang from the chair and grabbed me by the shoulders. "Is she all right? Is anything wrong?"

"She's seems to be fine. Why don't you go up to see her while I make her a cup of clover tea."

"Yes, yes, good idea. I need to tell her that her parents stopped by about an hour ago . . ." He bounded from the room and up the stairs, three at a time. I chuckled to myself as I searched through Sally's food stock for a tin of clover tea. Realizing I hadn't eaten since breakfast, I sliced and buttered a piece of Sally's homemade bread and ate it before returning to my patient.

Sally, Stan, and I watched the fireworks display from their bedroom window. I shuddered with each explosion, just as I had when I was a little child. But the greater terror was what would happen after the show ended—Emmett would come to drive me home. What would I do? After the last display of light and sound faded, I shooed Stan from the room while I helped Sally bathe and settle down for the night.

I heard Emmett's wagon pull up in front of the house and his knock on the front door. When Stan came up the stairs to get me, I looked about wildly for an escape. *One more time, God? Can You rescue me just one more time?*

My escape came from Sally. "Chloe, I hate to ask this, but would you be willing to stay the night? I'm still scared I'll lose this baby. We have a lovely guest room."

Relief flooded over me like a springtime thaw. "Well, I suppose I could stay. Pa or Joe could come for me in the morning." I turned to Stan. "Please tell Mr. Sawyer thank you for going out of his way for me, but Sally still needs me."

From the top of the stairs, I heard Stan deliver my message. Then the door slammed behind Emmett as he stormed from the house.

Later, in Sally and Stan's darkened bedroom, I contemplated Emmett's plan to tame me. I'd lived near a small town my entire life, so I knew his threats were real. A word here, a raised eyebrow there, and my reputation would be sullied forever.

Would my father defend me? What could he do? God had sent Amby along at the right moment, but could He control Emmett's vindictive nature? I wasn't sure. Through the curtains I looked up at the brightest star I could find. *Maybe this one's too big for both of you.*

The Ultimatum

The first rosy hues of dawn glowed in the eastern sky as Pa's wagon pulled up in front of the Kirkpatrick house. Unable to sleep, I had spent the night worrying about Emmett's threats. Hearing me tiptoe down the stairs, Stan came out of the master bedroom to thank me. I left instructions for him to send for me if Sally went into labor.

My father was coming up the front walk when I rushed from the house. "Pa, I'm so glad you came for me. I don't know how to tell you this, but—"

I sprang onto the wagon and waited for him to climb aboard and urge the horses forward. When I continued, he lifted his hand to silence me. "Before you say anything else, Ma and I had a long talk with Emmett last night, so I don't want to hear it."

"Hear what? That I don't want to marry him?"

"He said you'd say that. Look, Chloe Mae, it's normal for couples, married or just courtin', to have spats."

"Spats? Is that what he called it, a spat?" I snarled and turned away.

"You are a very lucky young woman. He's more than willing to forgive you for your immaturity."

"Forgive me?"

"Yes, forgive you. You could surely do a lot worse for

yourself, you know." He almost sounded convinced himself.

"I don't know how or where!" I jutted my chin forward and tapped my foot on the wagonbed.

A tone of finality crept into his voice. "Chloe, I won't discuss this with you while you're being unreasonable."

I didn't even try to hide the tears slipping down my cheeks. *How can I make him listen? He has to listen.*

My voice shook as I spoke. "Will you at least listen to my side of the story?"

He shook his head and urged the horses to go faster. "We talked everything over last night. As your mother pointed out, brides-to-be become flighty and skittish before their weddings. And we agree with Emmett that an August wedding is a good idea."

Panic prickled throughout my body, right down to my fingertips. I had to make him understand just how serious I was about my decision. "Flighty? Skittish? Next you'll say I'm hysterical and don't know what I'm doing." My voice climbed to a dangerously high screech. I paused to get control of myself. In a calm, measured tone, I said, "I won't marry that man, no matter what you or Ma say!"

One look at my father's face, and I knew I was in serious trouble. I'd said it all wrong. Challenging Pa's authority would not win me any battles, let alone a war. I needed allies, not adversaries. He halted the horses in front of the house. Before I could leap from the wagon, he grabbed my arm.

"Chloe, it's about time you begin thinking of others instead of yourself. I won't have you going in there and upsetting your mother further. What with Riley joining the army and Mr. Chamberlain changing Joe's departure date to tomorrow, she's a nervous wreck."

A sudden rush of blood pounded inside my brain.

"Joe? He's leaving tomorrow?"

"That's right. And Ma needs your help getting his clothes ready for the trip. She and Hattie are out back starting the wash already."

I hurried inside the house and up to my room. I threw the new yellow dress into a heap on my bed. Slipping into my everyday brown calico, I rushed downstairs to help my mother and sister. When I reached the backyard, I found that even Ori had been put to work hanging the men's socks on the fence pickets to dry.

While my mother scrubbed Pa's work shirt on the washboard, Hattie leaned over the washtub, wringing out a pair of Amby's patched dungarees, passed down from Riley and Joe successively. She pushed a stray lock of hair from her forehead and grinned. I looked away; the last thing I wanted at the moment was to have anyone see my pain. The smallest word of encouragement, and I knew I'd burst into tears.

I hurried over to the tub and edged my mother aside. "Here, let me do that. You need to rest."

She stepped back and dried her roughened hands on her apron. "Have you eaten anything yet this morning, Chloe? Can I get you something?"

Reluctantly, I turned to look at her. Concern filled her eyes. I sensed she was reaching out to me. "I could certainly go for a tall, cold glass of milk."

She broke into a relieved smile and hurried inside the house. I hauled a work shirt out of the water and scraped it across the washboard with all my might. It felt good to take out my anger on something. Again and again, I worked the shirt across the metal ridges of the board. Probably I would have scrubbed a hole in the collar if Hattie hadn't interrupted me.

"You're going to wear out that shirt before Pa does."

I looked down at the limp garment and laughed. If I'd

been scrubbing Emmett's head instead of Pa's shirt, he'd have been bald by the time I finished.

Although I'd been awake all night, I pushed myself throughout the day, volunteering for the worst tasks. Once I caught my mother staring at me with disbelief. When it came time to take the clothes off the line, I was out the door like a hornet. My frenzy continued into the late afternoon. With shoulder muscles aching, I stripped the family wash from the clothesline. I helped Ori collect the family's socks from the pickets. I folded Ma's camisole and placed it in the clothes basket, along with Hattie's and my crinolines. As I removed Amby's dungarees from the line and held them up to my waist in order to fold them, I discovered they were a perfect length for me.

A train whistle echoing across the valley turned my thoughts to Joe's departure the next morning for California. Then I remembered the young man I'd seen hopping the train the day my nephew was born. I glanced back down at the pants and frowned. "Don't be silly, Chloe Mae!"

Ori turned and asked, "Did you say something?"

"No, nothing, honey." I blushed, folded the dungarees, and dropped them into the basket. Once the lines were emptied, I carried the loaded baskets into the house. Ori tagged along behind. She had hundreds of questions about California and Joe's upcoming train ride. "I wish I were going," she said. "Someday I will, won't I, Chloe?"

"You bet, kiddo. Someday."

The aroma of Jacob's pottage, as my mother called her lentil stew, set my taste buds clamoring. I'd forgotten how long it had been since I'd eaten a regular meal. Hattie sat in the rocking chair, playing with Dorothy. I walked over to the sideboard and sliced off the heel from one of the freshly baked loaves of bread. "Where's Ma?"

"I sent her in to take a nap before supper. So, how did it go yesterday for Sally?"

"She'll be fine."

"Good! I was worried. First Myrtle, now Sally. It doesn't seem possible that either of them could possibly be old enough to be mothers."

As I removed the soup bowls and plates from the breakfront, I thought about Hattie and wondered about her dreams. She never shared them, at least, not with me. Her obvious love for the baby in her lap showed in her every action. Would she spend her life caring for younger brothers and sisters and never have little ones of her own? If only she hadn't broken her hip. If only she were the one Emmett wished to marry. Then I remembered his cruel behavior at the picnic. No, I wouldn't wish him on my kind and gentle sister.

I stacked the bowls on the counter beside the stove and distributed the plates around the table. "Thank you for helping Ma make my new dress, Hattie. Borrow it anytime you like."

She looked up from the baby. "Really?"

"Sure, why not?" I returned to the breakfront and opened the silverware drawer. "Hattie, may I please talk to you about Emmett and yesterday?"

My sister looked away. "I'd rather not."

I covered my face in my hands. The forks and spoons I'd been collecting clattered to the bottom of the drawer. "No one will listen. No one cares."

I knelt on the braided rug in front of the rocker. "Please, hear me out." I clamped my hand across my mouth to contain my sobs. "I'm so scared, Hattie. Mr. Sawyer is a cruel, vicious man. I can't spend the rest of my life married to such a person. And I don't know what to do."

Hattie placed the baby's spoon in the empty bowl and set it down beside the chair. "He said you'd say that."

I buried my face in my rumpled skirts. *What is this man trying to do to me? Isolate me from everyone who loves me?* Desperate, I sat up and unbuttoned the cuff on my sleeve, then pushed it halfway up my forearm. "He did this."

Hattie gaped at the ugly bruises on my wrist and arm, then at me.

"I hate to think what might have happened if Amby hadn't shown up when he did. Worse yet, he threatened to ruin my reputation if I didn't marry him."

Hattie set Dorothy on the rug, then dropped to her knees beside me. She ran her hand gently over my bruises. "You're going to have to tell Pa about this."

I winced. "He refuses to listen to me at all."

"Give him another chance."

My brothers bounded in from the barn before I could reply. I dried my tears on the hem of my dress and pretended to be playing with Dorothy. Hattie struggled to her feet. "You boys get cleaned up. Supper's almost ready. Is Pa home yet?"

"Yeah." Ten-year-old Jesse pumped a fresh supply of water into the wash basin sitting in the sink. "He and Joe are unharnessing the team. They'll be in shortly."

I stood up and looked at Hattie. "Maybe you're right. I'll be right back."

I found them in the tack room. As he tossed the harness on the bar, Joe threw me a sympathetic glance but didn't speak. My father headed for the door without a word.

"Pa, I must talk with you. Please . . ."

"Chloe, I've said enough." A muscle flexed in his cheek, the one Ma called his mulish muscle. "Emmett will be here later to say goodbye to Joe. Now let's not spoil your brother's last night at home."

"But, Pa . . ."

My father glared at me, then threw an arm around Joe's shoulder. "Come on, son, let's go enjoy a bowl of your ma's lentil stew."

I stayed in the barn until I heard the terrifying sound of mice scampering about me. The mice and the rumble of wagon wheels prompted me to dash for the house. I didn't want Emmett to find me alone in the barnyard.

As I slipped through the kitchen door into the pantry, I heard Pa's voice. "She's out in the barn pouting again."

It was followed by Hattie's gentle voice. "Pa, I think you should listen to her."

"Hattie, mind your own business. Your mother and I know what is best for Chloe."

"But, Pa . . ."

The wagon stopped out front of the house. I heard a chair scrape on the floor. "Enough! I am sick and tired of back talk. That's probably Emmett now. Jesse, go get your sister!"

I stepped into the kitchen. "That won't be necessary. I'm here." I sat down in my place at the table while my father answered the door. My stomach lurched at the sight of the bowl of stew in front of me. Earlier I'd been so hungry, but now . . . I pushed it away and headed for the stairs.

Before I could escape, Pa and Emmett entered the room, followed by his son, Charley. A smiling Emmett strode to my side, placed his arm about my waist, and whirled me about to face my family. I tried to shrink away, but he held me tight. I looked up in time to see a worried glance pass between Hattie and Joe. Only Pa refused to look my way.

"I suppose all of you know by now that Chloe Mae and I have set our wedding date—August. Too bad you won't be here, Joe. I know how important you are to my beautiful bride-to-be."

My younger brothers and my sister Ori cheered as Ma rushed over and kissed my cheek. "Be happy, my child," she whispered between sniffles.

Ma set two more places at the table, one for Emmett and one for Charley. Throughout the meal, Emmett pressed his leg next to mine. With Joe on the other side, I had no place to move.

After dinner, Hattie and I cleared the table while Ma served the cake she'd baked especially for the occasion. She bustled about the kitchen, chattering about how much she needed to do before the wedding. "If you like this cake, Emmett, I'll use the recipe for the wedding. It was my mother's, you know."

I could barely swallow a bite. I was relieved when, a few minutes later, Myrtle, Franklin, and the baby arrived. They'd come to say goodbye to Joe and to congratulate me on my engagement. At Ma's insistence, we moved into the parlor. Emmett led me to the sofa, sandwiching me between him and the armrest.

Joe sat next to the fireplace in a straightback chair he'd carried in from the kitchen. As he regaled everyone with tales about the Chamberlain family and their strange antics, I noted his excessive good humor and flushed face.

Without warning, the significance of the evening penetrated my distress. *He's playing a role, like a snake-oil salesman with a traveling sideshow—like I am.* Our eyes met and held for a moment. *He doesn't want to go to California any more now than he did the day he told me about the offer.*

Sobered by my discovery, I gazed about the family circle. We were all playacting—Ma, Pa, Hattie. While we laughed and talked about Joe's adventure, we harbored the same thought. First Riley, now Joe. When would we all be together again? Tears welled up in my eyes.

When I felt Emmett's arm around my shoulders, frustration replaced the poignancy of the moment. He drew lazy circles on my shoulder and neck. I wanted to swat him like I would a horsefly, but I couldn't ruin Joe's evening. Besides, a scene was exactly what Emmett wanted. The less mature he could make me appear before my parents, the less likely they would listen to me.

When the clock in the kitchen gonged nine, Pa stood up, reached into his back pocket, and drew out two shiny twenty-dollar gold pieces. Holding them up for all to see, he cleared his throat. "We're here tonight as a family to honor Joseph. Tomorrow he embarks on the road of adulthood. Son, it is my honor to pass on this coin to you from your grandfather." He handed the coin to Joe and gave him a bearhug.

Jesse, who'd been sitting on the floor next to Pa's chair, tugged at Pa's pant leg. "The other coin, Pa? Who gets the other coin?"

My father released Joe and gazed my way. "Why, son, this one goes to Chloe on her wedding day—the bride's dowry."

"Hear that, Charley, my boy?" Emmett grinned at his own son. "Looks like we'll get the new calf pen after all."

One look at my father's face, and Emmett realized he'd overstepped his position. "Just joshin' ya. Just joshin'."

Everyone laughed except me. I moistened my parched lips and tried to smile. He might be able to convince my parents he'd been joking, but I had no doubt the man was totally serious.

My father placed the second gold coin on the mantelpiece and turned to Joe. "Well, son, you'd better be getting to bed, or you might oversleep, and the train would leave without you."

With dread, I watched the family circle unravel before me. Franklin rose from the settee and shook Joe's hand. Ma held Myrtle's baby while Myrtle kissed Joe goodbye. He walked them out to their carriage. After they left, Emmett's son, Charley, thanked Ma for the supper and walked outside onto the porch.

Ma shooed Jesse and Amby upstairs to bed. Without a glance in my direction, Pa picked up the sleeping Dorothy from the floor and carried her from the room. With Ori on one side and Worley on the other, Ma followed. Hattie limped over to the parlor door and paused. Her sad eyes told me she'd been watching and understood.

"Good night, Hattie." Emmett smiled a smile of dismissal. The door closed behind her. He stood, took my hands, and pulled me to my feet. He ran a lazy finger along the edge of my face and under my chin. "You've been a good girl this evening, Chloe. Maybe you're going to be easier to break than I thought."

Don't count on it, buddy. His voice grew husky as he leaned forward. "It is altogether proper for a man to kiss his intended, now isn't it?"

I turned my face to one side. My teeth ground together in anger. "I'd rather die than allow you to kiss me."

My hands still trapped in his, he pulled me to him. "You'll live to regret those words, my dear."

His threat gave me the courage I needed. Burying my chin to my chest, I lunged forward with all my might. The move caught him off guard. He landed with a thud on the footstool in the center of the room. Before he could recover, I sprinted from the room. *Wrestling with older brothers has some benefits,* I thought.

I bolted out the front door and down the steps, past a startled Charley, who stood talking with Joe. Patches bounded after me, barking and leaping.

"Chloe," Joe called. "What's wrong?"

I kept running. My first thought was to head for the loft. But I knew that was the first place anyone would look. Circling the barn, I disappeared into the apple orchard. I stumbled over dirt clods, but kept running. I zigzagged between the rows of trees. I wanted to run and run and run until I couldn't run any farther. Where didn't matter, as long as it was away from Emmett Sawyer.

I ran until I tripped over a dead limb. *How far can you go? Sooner or later, you'll get tired. Then you'll have to walk all the way home.*

Slowly I rose to my feet and cracked my head against a low limb. Eyeing the limb speculatively, I hiked my skirt up around my knees and climbed the tree. Patches curled up by the base of the tree, as if waiting for me to come to my senses.

As I heard Emmett's wagon lumber past the orchard on his way home, I shifted my body so that he couldn't see me from the road. *This is silly—sitting in an apple tree in the middle of the night. You are acting as immature as Emmett claims. Either carry out your threat to run away, or go back home and face the music.*

Actually run away? How? Where? I shook the thought from my mind. Pa was right, a man could strike out on his own, but a woman? Hardly. I waited until the lights in the house went out, then climbed down from my perch and made my way back to the loft.

Patches whined for me to carry him up the ladder. I shushed him and sent him away. Of course he didn't go.

Instead of lighting the kerosene lamp, I felt my way

over to the window and released the shutter. The room filled with moonlight. Wrapping the quilt about me, I snuggled down in my hiding place. I had never felt so miserable or so alone. My eyes burned. My head ached.

First, I prayed for a miracle. Then I imagined all the dire accidents that could happen to Emmett. I didn't ask God to make something terrible happen, but I considered it.

I thought about Joe sleeping in his bed for the last time. Joe—my protector. I remembered the time Joe decapitated a rattler in the woodpile with one swing of the ax. Once when I was five, he helped me down out of a tree I'd climbed, and he never laughed at me. At school, he always rescued me from the bullies. But now, when I needed him most, he was on his way to California. About three thousand miles—far from Emmett . . .

I leaned against the barn wall and closed my eyes. Scenes of the last few days played across my mind in rapid succession—Pa, Joe, California, the drifter who hopped a boxcar, Emmett. Suddenly, a bolt of lightning hit me. *Far from Emmett . . .* California was certainly that—far from Emmett. *No, I could never . . .*

It wasn't as if I'd be totally alone—Joe would help me. I leaped from my hiding place, lighted the kerosene lamp, and turned the wick down low so no one could spot its glow from outside the barn. Perched atop Ma's trunk, I began to formulate a plan.

I'll stow away on Joe's train in the morning. I considered hiding in the company Pullman car but decided that would be too risky. Then I remembered the stable car. *If I hide under a pile of hay in one of the corners until the train's too far from Pennsylvania, Joe won't be able to ship me back home.*

I glanced down at my dress and grimaced; the hem was out where I'd caught it climbing out of the tree. *The dress will have to go. There's no way I can hop a boxcar wearing a skirt and three petticoats. Besides, people will notice a young woman loitering around a train station while they'd pay no mind to a boy.* Spying one of my father's worn-out, narrow-brimmed hats on a nail by the door, I grabbed it and stuffed my braids up under it—perfect. I admired my reflection in the windowpane. Then I remembered Amby's patched dungarees. *Yeah, the dungarees with one of Pa's old work shirts—I could pass for a boy, freckles and all.*

The Twenty-Dollar Gold Piece

Patches tagged at my heels as I crept out of the barn and across the yard to the kitchen door. Holding my breath, I unlatched the door. I exhaled gratefully—I'd half expected Pa to be angry enough to lock me out. Stepping inside the pantry, I bolted the door behind me and tiptoed up the stairs to my room. Once there, I shed my clothes and slid between the sheets.

"Chloe?" Hattie whispered in the darkness.

"Yes?"

"I understand. About Emmett, I mean."

"Thank you." I punched my pillow and squirmed, trying to get comfortable. I didn't want to talk with her.

"What are you going to do?"

My nerves tingled with excitement at the thought of my outrageous adventure. I wanted to tell her. Hadn't I shared every secret with her since I was a toddler? "I-I'm not sure."

"You'd tell me if you were going to do something foolish, wouldn't you?"

"The most foolish thing I can do is to go along with Emmett's plans," I sighed. "Whatever I choose to do, it will be better if you don't know ahead of time. Then Pa can't get mad at you."

"If that's the way you want it, fine!"

I hated shutting her out, but anything else would be even more unfair. Silence again settled over the room. I stared at the ceiling, wishing I could sleep. Tomorrow would be a long day, and I would need my strength. The minutes ticked away slowly. The mantel clock downstairs gonged on the half-hour, then the hour. I dozed off, only to be startled awake by the rooster crowing. Leaping from the bed, I hurried into my brown calico. Pa could wake up any minute, and all would be lost.

A crumbled heap on the floor beside the bed caught my attention—my new cambric dress. I picked it up and held it in front of me, the lace caressing my chin. Conflicting emotions played tug of war with my reason. Reason won out. My eyes watered as the garment slipped from my hands to the floor. *I'm sorry, Ma. Hattie will enjoy wearing the dress.*

I grabbed my hairbrush, hairpins, and a change of underclothes from my bureau drawer. At the last moment, I decided to take along my favorite blue shawl and my brown sun hat. As I passed the foot of the bed, Ori sat up and rubbed her eyes.

"Is it morning yet?"

I touched my fingers to my lips. "No, honey, just go back to sleep."

She smiled a warm, sleepy grin and lay down. For one last time, I studied her trusting face, a lump swelling in my throat. Taking a deep breath, I tiptoed past Hattie's bed without glancing her way. If she awoke and caught me leaving, I knew my resolve to run away would crumble.

The boards creaked as I inched my way down the staircase. When my toe touched the kitchen floor, the rooster crowed a second time. I pawed through the laundry basket until I uncovered Amby's dungarees and one of Pa's shirts, which I wrapped around my small bundle.

Suddenly my parents' bedstead groaned. I froze as I heard my father pad over to the chamber pot. My mind went blank. Frantic, I tried to remember what I'd planned to do next. *Food—enough to last for two days.* Two travel days should be far enough to secure my safety. I slipped into the pantry, found one of Ma's calico flour sacks, and dropped my bundle of clothes inside. Removing half a loaf from the bread box, I sliced it into four pieces, spread a thick layer of honey on each slice, and slapped the pieces together. Then I pried open the soda cracker tin and removed a handful.

I looked around for a moment. *What else?* I spied a pan of day-old johnnycake Ma had been saving for the chickens. I helped myself to four large pieces of corn bread. *Sorry, but I need this more than you.*

Stacking the food on the broad shelf, I looked for something in which to carry it. Jesse's lunch bucket would do just fine. I placed the food in the tin, along with three apples and two raw potatoes. I eyed the pickle barrel greedily, but decided that vinegar-saturated johnnycake and soda crackers would be less than appetizing. I placed the bucket on top of my clothes and knotted the top of the sack.

I froze once more at the sound of my parents' bedroom door opening. My heart pounded as I heard my father open the firebox on the kitchen stove. A split log thudded against the cast iron. I heard the swoosh of hot coals being stirred.

Waiting any longer would increase the risk. My fingers shook as I lifted the oak bar from its brackets.

I waited until I heard Pa go back into the bedroom and close the door. It was now or never. At this point, I could either sneak back upstairs to my bed and no one would ever know what I'd intended to do, or I could walk out the door. Before I could change my mind, I stepped outside into the predawn darkness.

A surprised yip filled the air. Patches leaped around my feet barking. "Ssh, ssh, Patches," I whispered. "Pa is gonna hear you."

A light appeared inside the house. It danced across the room and into the pantry. As I ducked around the corner of the house, Patches bounded against my skirt, coaxing me to play. Desperately I set my bundle down and held his muzzle closed with one hand and stroked his head with the other. "Good doggie. Good doggie. Ssh-ssh-ssh."

The back door creaked open. Pa leaned out, kerosene lamp in hand. I heard him call to Ma. "I could have sworn I heard the dog bark. Must have been chasing a squirrel."

As the door creaked shut, I exhaled slowly. After giving Patches one last warning, I picked up my pack. The wind whipped my unbraided hair across my face. *Oh, no, Pa's hat! I had left it in the loft.*

I hurried to the barn and climbed into the loft, deciding to change clothes while I was there. After removing my food cache, I dumped the rest of the contents on Pa's worktable. Shedding my brown calico dress and petticoats, I stuffed them into the bottom of the sack. First I slipped into Pa's shirt, then into Amby's baggy dungarees. I hauled them to my waist and buttoned them closed. Startled, I stretched the waist of the pants out six inches from my body. *How will I keep these things up? Twine, Pa always has a roll of twine around somewhere.*

I pawed through the shelves but could find no string, no rope, no twine—nothing. I opened Ma's trunk—yards of lace, a stack of letters, her wedding dress, a leather sack—Pa's gold coins. Beside the sack were a pair of leather suspenders. Draping the suspenders over my shoulders, I attached them to the pants, then wiggled about, tightening and adjusting to my comfort. They worked. I slammed the trunk closed.

Shaking with a delightful blend of excitement and fear, I brushed through my hair and worked it into one heavy braid. I pinned the braid into place and stuffed the awkward bump under Pa's hat, feeling around the brim to be certain the braid was hidden.

I picked up the quilt I kept stowed behind the trunk and folded it. A wave of panic swept through me as I glanced down at the pitiful little pile of possessions I'd chosen to take with me. A long list of "what ifs" that I should have considered earlier swept through my mind. That's when the thought that I might need money first crossed my mind. Then I remembered Pa's twenty-dollar gold pieces in the trunk.

Hmm, it wouldn't be stealing to take what is technically mine anyway, would it? Besides, what's the theft of a coin? I'd already stolen Amby's pants; Pa's shirt, suspenders, and hat; Ma's flour sack; and Jesse's lunch pail. Why I decided to pray at this point, I didn't know. Maybe I expected to be absolved for what I was about to do before doing it.

"Dear Father, I know it's a little late to ask for Your advice. But that twenty-dollar gold piece will help me more now than after I'm forever married to Emmett Sawyer. Please forgive me."

It only took a moment to open the trunk, locate the leather pouch, and extract one of the coins. The kitchen door slammed. I jumped, crashing the trunk lid down with a thud, barely missing my left hand. The coin pouch fell to the floor. If Pa and the boys came out to the barn to do the morning chores while I was still in the loft, my adventure would end. I leapt to my feet and stuffed the quilt and my other belongings, including one coin, into the flour sack and knotted the top.

I crept from the barn and darted into the orchard. It would be a long walk to town, but there was no other way. I jogged the length of the orchard, never once looking back. It wasn't until I'd clambered up the bank to the roadway that I noticed Patches trotting by my side.

"Patches, go home!" The dog barked, his tongue hanging out as if he expected me to play toss and fetch. I stomped toward him. "Patches, go home!" He backed off, crouching, eager for our game to begin. I picked up a stone and threw it. It caught him in the side. He yelped, his eyes filled with confusion. He couldn't understand why I'd hurt him; I'd always been his buddy.

A swift stab of remorse swept through me, and a sob escaped my throat. When I realized I might never see the dog again, I scooped him into my arms and saturated his black-and-white fur with tears.

"I'll miss you, little friend." Patches licked at my tears, instantly forgiving me for hurting him. "Please go back to the house. Please . . ."

I stood up. The dog cocked his head to one side, then trotted into the orchard. He stopped by the first tree and looked back at me, expecting me to follow. I hardened my heart against his hopeful gaze, wiped my tears on my shirt sleeve, and strode down the middle of the road. *I won't look back! I won't look back!*

My trip to town was one of dodge and hide. Whenever I heard a wagon coming, I'd leap behind a bush or into the ditch and pray that the driver would pass without seeing me. After crossing the bridge, I skirted Main Street, hiding in alleyways and behind water barrels whenever anyone came into view.

I reached the edge of the cornfield beside the station just as my brother-in-law strode into view. It was his job to open the train station. I charged between the cornstalks and dropped to the ground.

Once I was certain he was gone, I stood up and dusted my clothes. I spied the stock car, sitting on a siding at the far side of the station. The day before Joe had stocked the car with grain and hay and fresh water for the horses. I circled around back of the station, crouching low beneath each set of dusty windows. A stranger with shaggy gray hair sat on one of the wooden benches in front of the station, his head resting on his chest. Though he pretended to be asleep, I could feel his eyes watching me as I passed.

Panic rose in my throat. *He knows I'm a girl!* I stood up long enough to see my reflection in a windowpane. A corkscrew of hair had escaped the braid and dangled down the side of my head. I scooted across the main tracks and behind the dark-green stable car.

After stuffing the offending curl back under the hat, I leaned against the side of the railway car and closed my eyes. Once my breathing returned to normal, I tried the sliding door on the side of the car. It was unlocked, but it took both hands to slide it open. I picked up my pack and tossed it aboard, hopped inside, and slid the door closed behind me.

The partial light inside the car illuminated the area that would be my home for the next two days. A third of the car was separated into two stalls, each complete with a mound of fresh hay. A rail fence separated the stable area from the rest of the car. In the larger section, there was an end door, which allowed the stable hand easy access to the horses. I opened the door and peered out. *I could have climbed the stairs onto the metal platform instead of pulling myself through the side door.* I closed the door and continued my inspection.

Two pitchforks hung on one side of the door, and on the other, a rail upon which to hang the saddles and bridles. Four large oak water barrels were strapped to the wall on one side of the car. A pile of filled grain sacks leaned against the other, as well as a stack of additional hay. Finding a small piece of canvas behind a water barrel, I wrapped my flour sack in it, then stuffed the pack behind the second barrel.

I considered burrowing under the hay immediately instead of hopping the train once it was moving, then rejected the idea. All it would take was one horse to sidestep while boarding or for Joe to stab into the hay with one of his pitchforks. One would mean a crushed foot, the other a lacerated side. Either would end my journey before it began. By hiding my pack on board, I could more easily hop the train once it left the station.

I glanced about to be certain nothing had been disturbed. For all of my brother's easygoing nature, he was a perfectionist when it came to his horses. I opened the end door and eased down the steps. As my feet landed on the wooden crosstie, I heard a shout.

"Hey, you! What do you think you're doing?"

I ducked beneath the car and held my breath. On the main track, the man I'd seen napping by the station sped past, with a rail-yard worker in pursuit. Relieved he hadn't spotted me, I eased out of my precarious hiding place and sprinted across the main track and into the cornfield. I'd barely disappeared between rows of corn when the Chamberlains' shiny black lacquered carriage rounded the corner at the end of the field. Behind the carriage pranced the two perfectly matched Morgans.

I flattened myself on the ground and watched the

procession roll past. The carriage stopped beside the stable car, and Mr. Chamberlain, Cy, Phillip, and Joe climbed out. After Joe untied the horses from the carriage, two rail-yard workers appeared with a horse ramp. Once the ramp was secured, Joe and the horses followed the Chamberlain men up the ramp.

My stomach fluttered with excitement. It was really happening. Joe was going to California. And if all went well, I was too.

A switchman, carrying a long-handled wrench, strolled toward me, stopping directly in front of where I lay. Bending down, he adjusted a bolt on the rail. I held my breath as he studied the bolt, then stared down the track.

Suddenly the little hairs on the back of my neck tingled. I felt eyes watching me. Turning my head, I discovered my worst nightmare had come true. I found myself staring directly into the face of a brown field mouse. Two more watched from a safe distance. Stifling a scream, I forced myself to close my eyes and breathe deeply. *Oh, dear God*, I prayed silently, *make them go away!*

When the switchman ambled back down the track, I thumped my hand on the ground and hissed at my curious observer. He skittered back to his relatives. A few minutes later, we repeated the process.

While I maintained the standoff with what to me seemed like the entire rodent population of western Pennsylvania, I could hear the chatter of excited voices as the platform filled with people. It looked as if the entire town had come to see Cy and Joe off and to get a glimpse of what the newspapers called a mansion on wheels.

The train pulled into the station amid a flurry of billowing steam and resonating whistles. The black-

and-brass engine and coal car roared by, accomplishing two services for me. It blocked the view of the platform and scared away the mice. In large brass script, the letters on the side of the engine read "Erie."

I watched Joe and the Chamberlain men leave the stable car and disappear to the other side of the train. Seconds later, the yardmen removed the ramp and sent up an all-clear to the yardmaster. Signals flew from one end of the smoke-breathing monster to the other and back again. I froze as railroad crewmen ran back and forth not more than ten feet from me. The conductor turned toward me as a part of the train pulled forward to be switched to the siding. I buried my face in my arms and prayed he hadn't seen me.

Forward and back, forward and back, the train went through the series of maneuvers necessary for hooking up the stable car to its proper place in the lineup. Once the cars were reassembled on the main track, the yard workers disappeared from my view. Cinders fell all around me as I scanned the length of the train from the engine to the Pullman, twenty-one cars in all. The stable car was sandwiched between the last boxcar and the first passenger car, I assumed for easy access to the horses.

I imagined my family gathered about Joe at the far end of the station, saying goodbye and wishing him well. I wondered if the Chamberlains invited my parents to tour the Pullman car before the train left. I wondered if anyone in the family suspected where I was or what I was about to do.

I lay with my chin in my hands and waited for what seemed like hours as the workers loaded the freight on board. *At least, the activity around the locomotive keeps the mice at bay.*

Two brief clangs from the bell. I pictured the passengers scrambling aboard, my parents and Cy's parents kissing their sons goodbye. Last-minute doubts niggled at my resolve. *Oh, dear Father. Am I doing the right thing? Please, please, say I'm doing the right thing.*

The great engine snorted and chugged. Steam hissed from its sides. After the brakeman walked back toward the rear of the train, I inched closer to the tracks. I could make out every articulated gear and mechanism attached to the beast's belly. As gray smoke plumed from the stack, the massive iron pistons began to turn the wheels on the engine, and the ungainly beast chugged forward. I crouched beside the tracks, ready to spring forward. The only problem was, I didn't know when to make my move.

Identifiers rolled by on the sides of the first box cars—H & O, Pennsylvania, Santa Fe, Union Pacific, Lackawanna. *Now. Should I run now?*

The train gathered momentum, the cars rumbling, shaking the ground, deafening me with their thunder.

I glanced over my shoulder. The stable car loomed closer. Some instinct told me it was now or never, time to run or quit. At the memory of Emmett's smirking face, I exploded into action. Gravel splatted about my shoes. I paced myself alongside the train. Somewhere behind me, a workman shouted for me to stop, but I kept running.

As the stock car eased alongside, I leaped for the railing at the end of the car. My fingers wrapped around the grab iron, and I grasped it with all my strength. My legs flew backward. I felt like a pair of Pa's freshly washed long johns, flapping about in a brisk wind. My breath came in short, terrified gasps. Frozen with fear, I could neither move forward nor let go.

The sight of the approaching wooden trestle that spanned the river spurred me to action. While scrambling for a foothold, I wrenched one of my hands free from the grab iron. Hand over hand, I inched my way up the bar until one of my feet touched the car's bottom stair. I scrambled to safety just as the bridge's iron girders flashed by.

I leaned against the brass rail and sobbed. Through blurred vision, I watched my whole world fade into the distance. I glanced down at my whitened knuckles still clutching the bar. The enormity of what I'd done draped itself about me like a water-logged blanket. Nothing would ever be the same for me again. In spite of the mid-July temperature, I felt cold inside. My teeth chattered, and I began to shake.

Slowly, my breathing returned to normal. I would have a few minutes to compose myself before we reached Olean, the first stop. If I stayed on the platform, I would be spotted as we rolled into the station. I didn't want my presence discovered a few miles beyond the Pennsylvania border. I turned the knob and entered the stable car. The two horses eyed me suspiciously and snorted.

My growling stomach reminded me it had been some time since I'd last eaten. Retrieving my sack from behind the barrel, I loosened the knot and reached inside for the lunch bucket. In the process, my fingers touched the hard, textured surface of the gold piece. My hand jerked back as if I'd touched the top of Ma's cookstove. I located the bucket and took out an apple. The horses looked on greedily as I ate the fruit, including the core. Next I cleared a patch of hay away from the wall. After spreading out my quilt, I collapsed onto it and considered what my next move would be.

Miles to Go

The steady rocking of the train lulled me into a much-needed sleep. As the locomotive slowed at the Olean depot, I awakened enough to turn over in the hay. Since the Olean stop was only to take on passengers, I knew I could sleep undisturbed. Joe probably wouldn't check the horses until we reached Salamanca.

A rattle at the side door jarred me awake. I burrowed under the hay, leaving myself a small peephole. The door slid partly open. The conductor stuck his head in the car and looked around. "No hobos here, Smitty. That guy in Shinglehouse must have been mistaken."

I held my breath until the door slammed shut once more. I hadn't realized until the open door let in a blast of fresh, clean air just how hot and sticky it had become inside the stable car. My body dripped with sweat. I could only imagine how evil I must smell. The moment the train lurched forward, I threw off the hay and spread out on top of my quilt. I itched everywhere. I had hay in my hat, hay in my hair, hay down my shirt and pants, even in my high-button shoes. *You'll get used to it. You'll get used to it,* I told myself. *Never. Never!* I argued.

I leapt up and staggered over to the water barrel. After splashing the tepid water on my face and neck, I opened the lunch bucket and ate half a bread-and-honey sandwich. Hungrily, I eyed the other half. No, I needed to conserve my food supply. As I placed the bucket back in the flour sack, my hand brushed against the coin. Feelings of guilt washed over me once again. I let the sack drop to the floor beside me.

The air currents seeping in through the cracks in the wooden slat walls felt refreshing. Tossing my hat onto the hay, I opened the end door and stepped out onto the platform. Cows and horses grazed on the hillsides along the tracks. I watched a flock of blackbirds soar above a ripening cornfield. A young boy standing in his backyard waved. The engineer blew the whistle and roared past a small settlement. Before long we were on the outskirts of Salamanca.

Back inside, I glanced about the stable car, trying to decide whether or not I should bury myself in the hay or leave the car during the stop. As the train pulled into the station, I shoved my sack behind the water barrel and reshuffled the hay. Spying my hat half buried by hay, I grabbed it and stuffed my hair beneath it. Brushing strands of hay from my clothes, I opened the door and descended to the bottom step. When the train slowed to a crawl, I leapt off and darted behind a storage shed.

From the shadow of the busy depot, I watched the baggage men load the freight. I was so busy watching the activity, I failed to notice Cy walking toward me. Panicked, I pulled my hat rim farther down over my face. He paused less than ten feet from where I stood frozen and shouted, "You check the horses, Joe, while I get us some reading material."

My brother waved and bounded up the stairs into the stable car. A few minutes later, he came out and stood at the top of the stairs with his hands on his hips, looking first one direction, then the other. Scratching his head, he climbed down and strode to the rear of the train.

I waited until he was too far away to recognize me, then darted out from behind the building—smack into Cy and his armload of newspapers. The papers flew in every direction. I didn't dare stop to help him pick them up. Instead, I vaulted across a boxcar coupling to the other side of the train. As I ran, I could hear him shouting at me, "Hey, kid! Watch where you're going!"

I climbed back into the stable car without being seen. Within a short time, the train inched out of the station. I'd passed the first hurdle on my trip west. Throwing myself onto the hay, I shrieked with delight. "I did it. I did it. I did it." One of the horses whinnied at my sudden outburst.

My hat tumbled off into the hay. I laughed and rolled over to face the beast. "Sorry, Duchess—or whatever you call yourself. Didn't mean to disturb your meal."

Starting to feel accustomed to my quarters, I opened the side door and stretched out to watch the scenery roll past. As the train crossed the long wooden trestle spanning the Allegheny River, the sunlight glinted off the waters. I rested my head on my arms and closed my eyes to luxuriate in the refreshing breezes caressing my face. We stopped at the Jamestown station long enough to allow a small group of passengers to deboard, and we were on our way again.

An hour and a half later we arrived at the Erie, Pennsylvania, station. The rows of tracks in the busy train yard seemed to go on forever. I'd never seen so many boxcars, passenger cars, flatcars, and tankers. Workmen were busy everywhere. A train pulled in beside us and blocked my view of the yard. *Should I get out or stay put?*

Out! Definitely! I needed to get out—regardless of the risk. I buried my quilt beneath the hay, put on my hat once more, slipped through the end door, and joined the surge of passengers dashing for the depot lunch room. With less than ten minutes to eat, the hungry travelers shoved anyone who hampered their speed.

Our train added another ten freight cars before I returned. I examined the train carefully to be certain it was the right one. The luxury Pullman answered my question. I joined a rush of passengers and well-wishers on the station platform and inched my way over to the stable car. Glancing about to be certain no one was watching, I sprinted up the steps, then back down the other side. The end door was open enough for me to spot Joe inside, giving the horses fresh water. I flattened myself against the side of the car and forced myself to breathe.

I heard my brother call out, "Is that you, Cy?" Seconds later, he emerged from the car and bounded down the steps. He looked both ways, then headed back toward the Chamberlain Pullman. I clambered on board as quickly as possible; I didn't want any more close calls.

The horses glanced up from their feed trough, but kept on chewing. Watching them eat made me hungry enough to haul out my stash of food. I set my pack near the side door, uncovered the quilt, and spread it out next to the pack. The train whistle sounded. Steam from the engine raced past the car. Metal screeched against metal. And the wheels began to turn.

Ah, relief! I opened the side door a couple of inches and sat down. I'd just stuffed a piece of johnnycake in my mouth when the end door flew open.

"Aha! I caught you." Joe burst into the car and grabbed me by the collar before I could escape. "What do you think you're doing?"

He lifted me to my feet and shook me. I tried to speak, but fear and dry corn bread glued my tongue to the roof of my mouth. My hat fell to the floor, allowing my braid to tumble free.

"Huh? What? Chloe?" His voice raised to a broken squeal as he gawked at my face. "What in the world are you doing here? Pa and I looked everywhere for you this morning. What is going on?"

I tried to look away. He grabbed my chin and forced me to look into his eyes. I tried to jerk free of his grasp, but he tightened his hold. "Answers! I want answers. Now."

When I tried to speak, I showered him with corn-bread crumbs. I hiccupped painfully and gasped for air. He glared while I chewed and swallowed.

"Well?" He shook me by the collar again. "I'm waiting."

I knew I had to gain the upper hand, or I'd find myself on a freight train heading east for Shinglehouse. I adopted the tone of a schoolmarm. "Will you let go and stop bullying me?"

"I'd like to do a whole lot more than bully you." He released my collar. I fell into the hay. My usually gentle, sweet-tempered brother loomed over me like an avenging ruffian. "You still haven't explained yourself."

"Isn't it obvious?" I shook myself and adjusted my shirt collar. "I'm running away."

"Of all the . . ." The train lurched unexpectedly. He grabbed for the rail. "You have done some dumb things in your time, Chloe Mae, but this . . ."

My eyebrows knitted into a challenge as I thrust my chin forward. "What are you doing in here? Aren't you supposed to be riding in your luxury car? Won't Cy think you missed the train?"

My counterattack worked. Joe tried to defend himself. "He knows I'm here. I found the flour sack behind the barrel, but I never suspected . . . I told him I suspected someone was tampering with the horses." Joe shook his head and ran his fingers through his hair. "What am I supposed to do with you?"

I leapt to my feet and squared off against him. "I didn't ask you to do anything with me. I'm doing quite well on my own, thank you. I have everything I need right here."

"Except a ticket! You are breaking the law, you know." Joe rolled his eyes upward. "Obviously, I'm going to have to send you home when we reach Cleveland."

"You can do what you like, but I'll not go back home!"

"Whoa there . . ." Joe's expression softened. "We have a long ride to Cleveland, the next major stop. So, let's talk this out."

I lowered myself onto the quilt, careful to maintain an adversarial distance from my brother. He sighed and knelt down on the far end of Ma's quilt. "How do you breathe in here? It's sweltering."

I winked and slid the side door open another six inches. Cool air rushed in.

He leaned back and nibbled on a piece of hay. "All right, talk! Why did you do it? And where did you get those clothes?"

"Pa's hat, shirt, suspenders, and Jesse's work pants."

He looked down at my high-button shoes and laughed. "And your own shoes? I don't believe it."

I shrugged and pawed around in my sack. "My feet were too small to fit anyone else's." I handed him the lunch bucket. "Here, help yourself." I removed my hairbrush from the sack and unwound my braid. "Look, Joe, I am sorry, but I couldn't think of any other way to avoid marrying Emmett. You don't know what kind of man he is. He's mean." I ran my fingers through my braid and shook the hair free. "I tried to tell someone, but the only one who would listen was Hattie. When she talked to Pa, he told her to shut up."

Joe eyed me critically. "I'm listening."

With slow, deliberate strokes, I brushed out the snarls. "So, early this morning, I packed a few things in one of Ma's flour sacks and walked into town. And as the train pulled out of the station, I jumped on board the stable car."

His mouth dropped open. "You hopped a moving train? You could have been killed. What were you thinking?"

Tears welled up in my eyes. "I was desperate, Joe."

"When you didn't come down for breakfast, Pa and I looked everywhere. Since your clothes were there, we decided you were off pouting somewhere." He stared out at the blurring countryside and shook his head slowly. "The only part that didn't make sense was the missing gold coin. You did take the coin?"

I nodded and reddened. "I, uh . . ." What could I say? I had no defense. I worried a strand of hay between my fingers. "What are you going to do?"

"I don't rightly know. Perhaps when we get to Cleveland I'd better wire the folks so they can stop worrying. I don't like the idea of sending you home, since I have no guarantee you won't run away again." Joe scratched his head. "Maybe I can borrow on my salary to pay for your ticket to California."

"No . . ." *I hadn't planned it this way.* "No, this is my problem. I created it, and I must solve it."

"Chloe, I love you dearly, but . . ." His face filled with frustration. ". . . but what can you do? You're a woman."

I laughed aloud, and with both hands, flicked my hair behind my shoulders. "Thank you for pointing that out, in spite of my clothing."

"Speaking of your clothes. You did bring along something acceptable, I hope."

"Yes, I did. Though I have to admit, you guys have been holding out on us women. These britches are a lot more comfortable than our petticoats."

He snorted and rose to his feet. "It might be best if you wait here while I go talk to Cy. If the train should make any unexpected stops before I return, stay out of sight. And, please, make yourself more presentable before I return!"

As Joe exited the car, I set to braiding my hair once more. Satisfied, I smiled to myself. I'd won the first battle. I was buttoning the last button on the neck of my dress when a knock sounded at the door. Fearful it might be the conductor, I grabbed my bonnet and shrank back into the corner.

"Chloe, it's me." Joe opened the door a crack. "I have Cy with me. Are you decent?"

"I'm fine. You can come in." The two men stepped inside the car and closed the door.

"I don't believe it! When Joe told me you stowed away on board, I laughed in his face." Cy circled me, looking me up and down. I felt like a prized heifer.

I glared and turned to Joe. "Well? What's next?"

"I wired a message home to the folks to assure them you're all right."

"While we're moving?"

Cy gave me an amused grin. "Every train has a telegraph operator on board. It's the law."

Joe went on. "Cy has purchased a ticket from the conductor. You can travel with us in the company car."

"Excuse me." I held up my hand and waved it in front of my brother's face. Turning to Cy, I said, "First, thank you, Mr. Chamberlain, for the, uh, loan. I will repay you as soon as possible." Cy started to respond, but I waved him aside. "Second, since I am now traveling as a woman, I would prefer to ride in one of the passenger cars. Not only would it be unseemly for me to travel unchaperoned with two gentlemen, even if one of you is my brother, but my debt to Mr. Chamberlain will be significantly less if I ride in a passenger car."

Joe groaned and threw his hands into the air. "Chloe Mae, you are a mule of a woman! Why Mr. Sawyer would even want to marry you is a mystery to me."

"Miss Chloe," Cy purred, "you don't know how uncomfortable those passenger cars can be. In our car, you'll be as snug as a bug in a rug."

"Waiting to be stepped on," I mumbled. At this moment, something in Cy's attitude reminded me of a younger Emmett. "I thank you again, Mr. Chamberlain, for the offer. And I will repay you for your generosity. But I prefer to do this my way. Now, shall we go?"

While Joe grabbed my flour sack, Cy offered his arm. "You are a most amazing woman, Miss Chloe." He escorted me through the dining car, two sleeper cars, and on through the first four, smoke-filled passenger cars. He opened the door to the fifth passenger car and turned toward me. "I think this will suit your needs, Miss Chloe."

I glanced about and nodded. It was the only one of the passenger cars smoke free and containing female travelers—eight in all. Cy led me to an empty seat and bowed. "May I have the pleasure of your company this evening for dinner? And before you ask, yes, your brother will be present."

I smiled and tipped my head politely. "Thank you. I accept your kind invitation, Mr. Chamberlain."

He nodded. "Very good. And now, if you'll excuse me, I'll leave you to your brother's capable care."

Joe lingered a few minutes longer. "You'll be all right alone, won't you? I can come back and ride with you, if you prefer."

I took my brother's hands in mine. "Joe, remember, Cy's father is paying you to keep track of that rogue. I'll be fine, honest."

"I still wish you'd reconsider riding with us in the . . ."

"I'm happy here. Now, go, I want to take a nap." I gave him a little push. "See you later this evening."

As the door closed behind my brother, I settled down into the upholstered horsehair seat. I was luxuriating in the comfort when the woman across the aisle called to me. A joyous grin wreathed her face.

"Are you traveling alone, honey?" Wisps of graying hair formed a frizzled halo around her face. A blue calico bonnet rested on her back. As much as I would have preferred napping to talking, I couldn't resist the eagerness in her twinkling blue eyes.

I looked over and smiled. "No, my brother's with me."

"Oh, that was your brother? How nice." The generously padded woman had received all the encouragement she needed. Patting her snoozing husband on the knee, she staggered across the aisle. The knitting bag looped around her wrist clattered against the wooden armrest as she fell into the empty seat.

"I don't think I'll ever become sure-footed on a moving train. We're Bertha and Conrad Schnetzler. We're heading home to Wisconsin after spending a few weeks with our son and his family in Schenectady, New York. So where are you going?"

"California. My name's Chloe—Chloe Spencer."

"California? My goodness child. Imagine, California." She settled back into the seat and folded her hands across her stomach. "What are you going to do in California?"

"Well, I'm not sure yet." I wondered if I should tell her about China. Would she laugh? "So, was this your first trip to New York?"

"Oh my, no." She patted a wiry lock of hair back into place. "My son William's a banker, you know. He and his wife, Laura, sent us round-trip tickets so we could see their firstborn son, William, Jr."

She chatted on about the baby with the same pride I'd heard in Pa's voice when he held Myrtle's baby, Franklin. My eyes misted. I turned my face toward the window.

"God has been so good to— Oh, but I do talk on, don't I?"

I glanced at my traveling companion. "You have a right to be proud of your grandchild. You say you own a farm in Wisconsin?" I rifled through my memory for everything I'd ever heard about the state. "A dairy farm?"

"Oh, yes. We own forty-five milkers. My younger son Horace is caring for them until we get back." Bertha rambled on about life on the dairy farm. She told how thirty years before they had left their homeland in Germany as newlyweds, traveled to the Midwest, and purchased and cleared the farmland. "We raised four sons together. They're grown and married now. Duncan's the oldest, then Carl. They both live near Milwaukee. And last, Horace owns a dairy farm near ours."

The woman dug into her knitting bag, pulled out a paper fan, and waved it before her flushed face. "Yes, over the years, God has been good to us. And how about you, dearie? Is Joe your only brother?"

"Hardly. We come from a large family." I don't know whether it was an unexpected wave of homesickness or Mrs. Schnetzler's insistent compassion. But once I started talking about my home and family, I couldn't stop. I told her about Hattie's accident, Joe's job in California, and my mother and her latest pregnancy. I babbled on about Riley's enlistment, and each of my brothers and sisters. When I mentioned Pa, a hollowness settled in my chest. I choked back my emotions.

It seemed only natural to tell her about my dream to go to China and about the cad, Emmett. When I mentioned that I'd run away, she shook her head sadly, all the while listening and patting my arm. Her gentleness brought tears to my eyes.

The woman reached into her large knitting bag and handed me an embroidered handkerchief. "Here, darling. Don't be ashamed to cry. God sends tears to cleanse the soul."

That did it. Any control that I had over my emotions melted away as the overwhelming seriousness of my decision to run away struck. She wrapped her ample arms about me and let me sob onto the bodice of her traveling dress.

"It's all right. Just cry it out. It's all right." She rocked me back and forth like I'd done so many times with baby Dorothy and with Ori.

Flustered and embarrassed, I finally pulled away and mumbled, "I can't believe I'm doing this. I don't even know you, and I'm baring my soul to you."

"Don't be embarrassed." Bertha smiled and brushed a stray curl from my forehead. "God knew you needed someone today. He placed me here to encourage you. We were supposed to take an earlier train, you know."

I frowned and eyed her suspiciously. "You don't believe God rescheduled your trip, do you? Do you honestly think the One who lives up above the clouds somewhere cares that I ran away from home today?"

Bertha looked at me in surprise. "I do, with all my heart."

I wadded and unwadded the linen handkerchief in my hands. "I find that difficult to accept. It's all chance. I didn't decide to run away until early this morning."

Her double chin quivered when she chuckled. "You are very special to God, Chloe dear. In Deuteronomy, He calls you the 'apple of his eye.'"

I'd never heard anyone take this religious thing so seriously. Not even Pa confused Scripture with everyday problems. "Don't get me wrong, you're a nice lady and all, but—"

"Chloe, there are no buts about it. God loves you with an everlasting love. He vows in His Word that He will never leave you, and He will never forsake you."

In my imagination I could see Pa sitting at the supper table, leafing through the family Bible. "Where does it say that?"

"Many places. My favorite text is in Hebrews 13:5. It says, 'Let your conversation be without covetousness; and be content with such things as ye have: for he hath said, I will never leave thee, nor forsake thee.'"

I thought back to the unanswered prayers I'd said over my patients. Where was He when I held a stillborn in my hands and ached to breathe life into its tiny body? Where was He when a young mother, barely twenty years old, died of consumption? "I'm sorry, Mrs. Schnetzler, but I can't accept that."

Bertha knitted her brow thoughtfully. "What do you believe about God?"

I thought for a moment. No one had ever asked me such a difficult question. "I guess, I think He's a great man who created the world and everything in it. But once He finished the job, He was finished. Now humans are on their own to make it work."

"Some people do believe that." She mulled my answer. "However, I would find it hard to believe God would go to the trouble to make people in His own image, then not want to be around to help His creation learn to 'walk,' so to speak." Her eyes shone as she spoke. "As a mother, I would have hated to miss seeing my son hold his son in his arms. It doesn't stop now that my children are grown and have young-uns of their own. I still want to share in their joys and in their sorrows."

"And you think God is like that?"

She chuckled. "I know it."

I liked this simple woman and her simple faith. If I had the chance to create a god, the one she described would be my choice. "You make it sound so reasonable. I would like to believe."

"You will, child. One day, you will." The woman smiled patiently. "God is touching your heart right now, even as we speak. He has a purpose for you. And He'll reveal it to you, in His time."

"And His purpose for you today was to comfort me?"

Her vibrant blue eyes captured mine. "That's right. Remember, you and I aren't accidents of nature. We're each part of His overall plan."

I sent her a devilish grin. "Then it must be in God's plan for me to run away to China."

She tapped my arm gently. "I didn't say that, Chloe. In my experience, running away seldom solves anything. Besides, God has the answer to our problems if we won't run ahead of Him."

"So you think I shouldn't have left home?"

The woman shook her head and smiled sadly. "Whether or not you made a mistake is between you and God. But even if you did make a mistake, He won't give up on you. He still loves you and cares for you."

The train whistle preceded the conductor's announcement of our arrival in Cleveland. "There will be a fifteen-minute meal stop. Please have your tickets ready when you reboard." He stopped beside my seat and handed me a sheaf of tickets. Without a word, he moved down the aisle and into the next car. Mr. Schnetzler snorted and cleared his throat. "Huh? Where are we? Bertha, where are you?"

"Right here, dear." Mrs. Schnetzler patted my hand once more, then moved back across the aisle to her own seat. "We'll talk more later."

Meet Mary McCall

Red brick buildings lined the track as the train slowed on the outskirts of Cleveland. Soon the train stopped, and passengers streamed out of the cars. When my turn came, I hopped down onto the wooden platform and stretched. It felt good to get out and walk around without slinking from shadow to shadow. I tagged along behind Joe as he checked with the telegraph agent to see if Pa had answered his telegram. He hadn't. While Joe sent a second wire, I headed for the ladies' rest area.

It felt good to brush the hay fragments out of my braids. Since I hadn't thought to bring along ribbons, I tore twelve inches of ruffled embroidery from the hem of my slip and tied my hair back into place. I pinched my cheeks pink for color. Tossing my flour sack jauntily over my shoulder, I twirled about in front of the gilt-framed wall mirror for one last check before entering the waiting area.

Cy leaned against a wooden pillar reading a newspaper. My brother was nowhere in sight. Cy's brown eyes twinkled with amusement when he saw me. *Is he laughing at me?* I patted my hair and bodice. *No, everything seems fine.* I straightened my shoulders and tipped my head toward him.

He ambled over to me, took my sack in one hand, and

extended his other arm. "Are you ready to dine, Miss Spencer?"

My stomach growled a reply before I could speak. I blushed. It had been hours since I'd eaten. When we strolled across the wooden platform, heads turned as we passed. I lifted my chin a notch. A porter greeted us at the steps of the private coach and relieved Cy of my flour sack. When Cy took my elbow and assisted me up the steps of the car, I felt like the queen of Bavaria.

Joe bounded up the steps behind us. "The horses are fine." He leaned over my shoulder. "So, what do you think?"

I looked at Cy, then at my surroundings. Both young men were eager to enjoy my reaction to the "mansion on wheels." As much as I might have wanted to disappoint them, I couldn't. Nothing had prepared me for the luxury I saw. I gaped at the splendor. Dark rosewood paneling with inlaid designs of light oak gleamed in the car's semidarkness, a bold contrast to the stark white linen tablecloth. Mahogany chairs with petit-point seat and back upholstery lined the perfectly appointed table. Even Ma's silver tea set from Ireland couldn't match the dazzle of the fine bone china and silver tea set under the gaslights. Fan-folded napkins blossomed out of the crystal stemware at each table setting. A bowl of fresh tea roses sat in the middle of the table. Though only three places were set, the table seated eight.

Cy pointed toward the front of the car. "This is the private dining room. Through that door is a fully equipped kitchen and pantry." We stepped from the dining area into a narrow corridor. He threw open the door of the first of four private sleeping rooms. "See, we have plenty of sleeping space."

Each room had a lower and upper berth with an enameled tub and bath between the two rooms. "The arrangement is the same on the other side of the aisle."

Impatiently Joe pushed by us and opened the door at the end of the corridor. "Wait until you see the parlor and observation lounge. They're my favorites."

I smiled. Joe was never one given to hyperbole. I paused at the doorway of the parlor. He'd not exaggerated the beauty of the room. Mirrors alternating with rosewood panels and heavily draped windows lined the walls of the parlor. Blue velvet draperies had been caught back with matching ties. My hand lingered on the back of a maroon velvet upholstered chair. The light from shaded gas wall fixtures glinted off the white marble-topped tables at each end of the maroon brocade sofa.

"This you're gonna love, Chloe." My brother grabbed my hand and dragged me to the far end of the car. The bemused Cy followed. Joe pushed me through the doorway. I didn't hear Cy join us.

The sight took my breath away. The side windows extended from a little lower than waist high up to and almost over the ceiling. A panel of rosewood ran down the middle of the ceiling between them. It was like riding in the open. *The view must be incredible at night*, I thought.

The train whistle blew, and the vehicle lurched forward. I reached for a bench to steady myself and felt Cy's hand on my waist. "Here, let me help you."

I turned and smiled.

"Chloe, don't miss this," Joe called from the platform at the far end of the coach. I hurried to his side in time to watch the city of Cleveland unravel behind us like a knitted scarf. Clouds in the sky behind the city reflected the pinks and mauves of the sunset as our train carried us west.

I continued to watch as overhead, the evening star

twinkled through the gathering twilight. I sensed Cy standing behind me, watching me. Even though I knew he might think I was acting like a small-town yokel, I didn't care. I didn't want to miss a thing.

When the white-coated servant announced dinner, I reluctantly returned with Cy and Joe to the dining room. "Is that man a real live butler?" I whispered to my brother after we were seated at the table. I'd only read about such people in books. Joe nodded and reached for the napkin in his goblet.

Cy leaned across the table toward me and whispered, "Acts kind of stuffy, huh? My mother would love him." I felt heat flooding my ears and neck. I hadn't planned on being overheard.

Cy's good manners and grace relaxed me in minutes. The three of us laughed, ate, and talked our way through six courses of what Cy called French cuisine. My host laughed as I rolled the strange names of the dishes around on my tongue—hors d'oeuvres, bordelaise sauce, potatoes Parisienne. When the butler removed our dinner plates, I leaned back and sighed. I was certain I couldn't eat another bite.

"You won't want to miss dessert," Cy warned. "We have mousse chocolat and crème Napoleon."

I choked. "Moose? Like fur and antlers?"

The butler interrupted before Cy could clarify. "Mr. Chamberlain, the conductor would like a word with Miss Spencer."

"What?" Cy looked irritated. "I took care of the ticket business."

"It's not that, sir." The butler bowed obsequiously toward Cy. "It seems there's a medical emergency in one of the passenger cars. Another passenger suggested that Miss Spencer might be of service."

"Miss Spencer? What could she—"

"An emergency? What kind of an emergency?" I pushed back the chair and jumped to my feet.

The conductor stepped inside the car. "A young woman seems to be going into early labor. A passenger, Mrs. Schnetzler, said you have delivered babies?"

"Yes, I have, but wouldn't it better to stop the train and get her proper medical attention, at a hospital, perhaps?"

The conductor looked at me down the length of his narrow, aristocratic nose. He seemed to be deciding whether to treat me with disdain or deference. "That is what I suggested, ma'am, but the young lady insists she is experiencing false labor pains, that it's not time for the child to arrive. I need you to verify her condition for me."

I dotted my face with the linen napkin and tossed it onto the table. "I'll be back." I glanced at the crestfallen Cy. "Save my moose for me, and one of those emperors too."

He laughed. "You mean a Napoleon?"

"Whatever . . ." I followed the conductor to the passenger car where the mother-to-be lay stretched out across two seats. Mrs. Schnetzler sat in the window seat facing the woman, comforting her. Across the aisle from the patient, a woman with frizzy blond hair held a small sniffling boy in her arms. The boy, dressed in western clothing, looked up at me, his eyes wide with terror. As I slipped into the seat beside Mrs. Schnetzler, curious onlookers craned their necks to get a better view.

"Chloe, dear, I'm so glad you came right away. Meet Mary McCall. Mary, this is the midwife I told you about."

Mary glanced up at me and frowned. "You're awfully young, aren't you?"

"Yes, but I'm getting older by the minute." The joke slipped naturally from my tongue. My apprehension gave way to experience. "Mary, why don't you tell me what you're feeling?" I leaned forward and untied the bow at the young woman's neck and handed the fashionable bonnet to Mrs. Schnetzler. I took the woman's wrist in my hand to feel her pulse. "How far along is your pregnancy? And what are you doing traveling on a train in your condition?"

"I'm barely seven months pregnant. I need to reach my husband in Kansas before this baby's born." The woman's face contorted with anxiety.

"It's all right. Take your time. Maybe it's a false alarm." I knew I had to check her thoroughly, but I could hardly do so with an audience. The conductor stood beside me, his face as impassive as if he were serving tea at a ladies' garden party. "Sir, could you tell my brother, Joe Spencer, that I need him, please?"

The man nodded and pushed his way down the aisle. Joe was there in minutes, Cy with him. "Mr. Chamberlain, could I place Mrs. McCall in one of your spare sleeping rooms? We need a little privacy."

Cy nodded. Together Joe and Cy lifted Mary into their arms.

"Wait!" Mary cried. "Jamie? Where's my Jamie?"

"Jamie?" I glanced toward Bertha Schnetzler.

In a burst of silent energy and flailing fists, the little boy from across the aisle broke free from the blond woman's arms and pummeled Cy's legs.

Cy backed away from the small child's blows. "Hey, what in the . . ." I lunged for the boy. But holding onto his tense, wriggling body was like trying to wrestle an angry barn cat.

I scooped the boy into my arms, trapping his little arms in my grasp. "Calm down, cowboy. No one's gonna

take your mama away from you. You're coming too."
The child's breath came in short gasps. I asked Mrs.
Schnetzler to gather Mary's belongings and to come and
help. She readily agreed.

"I really appreciate your helping me like this, Mrs.
Schnetzler."

"Please, Chloe, call me Bertha. I guess God had more
than one reason for putting you, Conrad, and me on this
particular train, huh? Quite a coincidence, wouldn't you
say?"

Having my hands full with the child, I cast her a wry
smile and hurried toward the Pullman. The men settled
the patient into a berth, and I handed Jamie to Joe,
suggesting he and Cy take the child on a tour of the
observation room. Then I asked the butler to bring us a
pot of chamomile tea.

Bertha seconded my request. "I swear by chamomile
tea. It soothes the nerves."

While I undid the top buttons of Mary's bodice, Bertha filled the porcelain basin with cool water. I removed
Mary's shoes and stockings. Bertha moistened a towel
and dabbed the cool water on Mary's face and neck.
When the butler returned with the hot brew, I helped
Mary sit up enough to drink it. Between sips she answered my questions.

"It's been a difficult pregnancy from the start. That's
why I stayed behind with my parents when James and
his brother, Ian, went west in March. I've been feeling
so much better these last few weeks that I thought it
would be safe to make the trip."

Mary leaned her head back against the snowy white
pillow. "Before we had Jamie, I lost three babies, you
know—all boys. James used to say he wanted ten sons
as strong as English oak trees." At the mention of her
husband, the tension her face showed eased. She told

about both of their families in Boston, Massachusetts. "Our fathers sold their estates in Scotland and emigrated to the United States when James and I were in our teens. You know, I knew since I was six years old that James would one day be my husband."

The tea did its trick. The contractions lessened, and Mary fell asleep. Later Cy returned to tell us that Jamie was asleep on the berth in the next compartment. Bertha suggested we take turns caring for Mary during the night. She offered to take the first watch.

"You don't know how soon Mary might be needing you. And as you said, you didn't sleep much last night."

I didn't need convincing. I slipped into the sleeping room next door. Someone had retrieved my sack from the Pullman's dining room and turned down the bedding on the lower berth. Snuggled into a ball at the foot of the bed was Jamie.

I closed the door behind me, unbuttoned my shoes, and kicked them into the corner next to the child's smaller, shinier pair. I wriggled my toes. Every muscle in my body ached from exhaustion. Totally forgotten were the mousse and Napoleon the butler had saved for me. I fell onto the berth and closed my eyes.

A sudden wail filled the air. Bolting upright, I found myself wrapped in total darkness. *Where am I?* The gentle rocking of the train and the clatter of wheels on steel rails helped me focus. A second scream sent me scrambling on hands and knees for my shoes. I heard the knock on the door an instant before it flew open. Bertha's shadow filled the doorway. "Chloe, you'd better come right away. Mary's in trouble."

The whimper at the end of the bed reminded me that Jamie must have awakened too. "It's all right, honey. Go back to sleep," I whispered, caressing his sweaty brow.

Bertha tapped my shoulder. "Chloe, hurry!"

I abandoned my search for my shoes and rushed to Mary's side. Instantly I knew this baby had no intention of staying put for another two days, let alone another two months. My only question was, in which state would the little rascal be born—Ohio, Indiana, or Illinois. I tried to speak, but the words stuck in my throat; then the memory of Auntie Gert's calm, relaxed voice took over. Quietly, I gave orders to the crowd gathered outside Mary's compartment.

"Cy, I need boiling water, clean linens, towels, lots of towels." Clearly apprehensive, Cy nodded after each item I requested. "Joe, take Jamie to your compartment and stay with him. He seems to trust you. Bertha, bathe the sweat from Mary's face and neck while I measure her contractions." A nagging fear gnawed inside me as I studied Mary's slight frame. *The woman's too weak to make it through this delivery.*

"I'm scared," Mary gasped between contractions. "I'm scared I'm going to die and never see James again."

Bertha bathed Mary's forehead. "Now, let's not borrow trouble from tomorrow. This baby needs every bit of strength you have. Let's just take this one contraction at a time, Mary. Try to relax between the pains. Hold Bertha's hand if you like. That's it, that's it," I soothed.

Just before dawn, the small, mewling infant arrived. I handed the girl child to Bertha to cleanse while I saw to Mary's needs. When Bertha returned, she placed the child at Mary's side.

"Oh, she's darling," I cooed. I ran my fingers over the hand-embroidered flannel blanket. "The blanket is so soft. Where'd you get it?"

"The conductor arranged to have one of Mary's trunks moved into the parlor. The blanket was right on top," Bertha explained.

The new mother gave her daughter a weak smile, then turned her head toward the wall and closed her eyes. I paused and gazed down at the sleeping pair, savoring my favorite moment of the birthing process. That's when I heard a soft, almost imperceptible purr coming from the baby. I placed my hand gently on the newborn's chest and felt a tiny rattle as she breathed in and out. When the baby hadn't bawled at birth, I had wondered. But the bluish tinge to her skin had so quickly changed to pink that I forgot about it. Now I looked at Bertha and frowned. She shook her head slowly, then gathered up the soiled linen and hurried from the compartment.

I also worried that Mary had lost an inordinate amount of blood during the delivery. I didn't know whom I worried about more—the mother or the newborn.

When Bertha returned, I asked her to care for the infant while I saw to Mary. The woman lifted the child tenderly into her arms and left the room. Noting the absence of color in Mary's face, I touched her brow. Her skin felt dry, like an autumn leaf about to crumble. She opened her eyes. "Chloe, I'm not doing too well, am I?"

"Of course you are. Don't be silly." I puttered about the tiny cubicle, avoiding her gaze. "You have a beautiful little girl. What do you plan to name her?"

She lifted her hand a few inches off the bedding, then allowed it to drop again. "I-I-I, listen to me. There are things I must ask you . . ."

Gently, I touched the side of her face with the back of my hand. "Mary, don't—"

"Please listen. During the night, Mrs. Schnetzler told me a little about your circumstances." She sighed, then continued. "I know this is asking a lot, but would you consider traveling with Jamie and me to Kansas to help with the baby? I'll pay all of your expenses. I have plenty of money."

Because I was thinking in terms of hours, not days, I brushed off her suggestion. "Well, let's see how things are in the morning when we reach Chicago. It might be better to get you to a hospital."

She shook her head from side to side on the pillow. "There's nothing they can do to help me that you cannot do." She placed her hand on my arm. "Please, at least consider my request. I'll pay you whatever you wish. I just know I'm not strong enough to make the trip with a five-year-old and a newborn."

"Mary, you've got to rest. Will you try to sleep if I tell you that I'll think about it?"

She smiled and closed her eyes. I slipped out of the sleeping compartment and made my way to the observation car. Bertha sat on one of the sofas, holding the sleeping baby. "How is Mary doing?" the woman mouthed silently.

I shrugged, then whispered, "I'm afraid Mary might be too weak to nurse. What will we do?"

"The butler and I are working on the problem. In the meantime . . ." She lifted a small, moist pouch from the baby's chest. . . . "I cut a square of cotton gauze from one of my slips and had the butler bring me some granulated sugar. Then I filled the pouch with the sugar and tied it off with a piece of yarn. It might not be Mommy, but it pacified her temporarily."

I laughed. I'd seen my mother do the same thing whenever one of her babies was colicky. Bertha laid the baby in a large lunch basket Cy had found in the kitchen. The baby stirred. Bertha patted its stomach gently. "Maybe if Mary sleeps for a while, she'll regain enough strength to begin nursing."

I knelt beside the baby and caressed her tiny fingers.

"And if she doesn't?"

The rumpled woman rested her head against the back of the sofa. "Mrs. McCall says she has plenty of money. We'll need to find a wet nurse for her, I suppose."

"What I need is to get Mary into a hospital or a boardinghouse where she'll receive proper—"

"A hospital? Have you ever seen inside a city hospital? It's where you go to die." Bertha shook her head. "And a boardinghouse would be worse. No one would take the time to care for a stranger, a little boy who doesn't speak, and a newborn baby, yet unnamed."

I knew she was right. My father had told horror stories of the hospitals in Pittsburgh that he'd once visited. I stood up and walked back to the door separating the parlor from the observation lounge and pressed my forehead against the wood paneling.

"Tell me, where will we find a wet nurse who would be willing to travel with Mary to Kansas?" No answer came.

I pressed my fingers against my aching forehead. "I'd better get back to Mary. Why don't you rest while the baby is sleeping?"

I sat on the floor beside Mary's berth throughout the night. She slept in short, fitful segments. During one of her waking moments, she announced the name of the child. "I've decided to call her Agatha Melvina, after James's and my mothers."

"Agatha Melvina."

"Melvina is a fine Celtic name, you know."

I tried to think of something nice to say. "Your mothers will be pleased, I'm sure. Agatha Melvina." Satisfied with my response, Mary closed her eyes and drifted back to sleep.

Agatha Melvina. I shuddered and closed my own eyes. *Poor child!*

I must have slept for a short time, for I awakened at the sound of someone calling my name.

"Chloe?" Mary stared down at me, her face wreathed with apology. "I'm sorry for waking you, but I'm frightened. I just know I'm going to die. Can you find my Bible in my portmanteau and read to me?"

I rubbed my eyes and opened the large travel case at the foot of the berth. There on top I found a Bible. I opened to the dedication page and read, "To my dearest wife, Mary Elizabeth Bradley McCall, from James Edward McCall on our wedding day, June 11, 1890."

She asked me to read Psalm 91. It took a while, but I found the chapter she requested. After I finished reading, Mary urged me to talk about my home and family. "Mrs. Schnetzler said you are traveling light."

I thought about my flour sack—the sum of my earthly possessions—and laughed. "One might say that."

"Then you must be needing changes of clothing. Help yourself to anything in my trunks. Bertha said the porters brought one of them into the parlor."

I demurred. "I wouldn't feel comfortable doing that."

Mary frowned and propped herself up on one elbow. "I insist. It's the least I can do after all you've done for me. Go out to the parlor and have one of the men bring the steamer trunk in here." To calm her, I agreed.

The butler's face remained impassive as he dragged the giant metal trunk into the tiny compartment. He stood the trunk on end and opened it for me. On one side of the trunk, clothing hung on specially designed hangers. The other side held six fabric-covered drawers. I stared at the gorgeous array of garments. Midnight blue, rose pink, creamy white, sage green, russet red, saffron yellow—I couldn't believe my eyes.

Mary pointed to the trunk and commanded, "Hold the russet silk one up in front of you." I obeyed. "That one, definitely. It sets your hair aflame. And the sage green lawn, yes, the sage green. Lawn is such a cool fabric to wear on a frightfully hot summer day."

She insisted I try on the two frocks immediately. Her face glowed as I stepped out of my brown calico and slipped the russet gown over my head. I buttoned the last of the tiny pearl buttons at the lace collar, then put on the matching bolero jacket that ended just above the gown's pinched waist.

Mary clapped her hands with pleasure. "It's beautiful. That dress never looked good on me anyway. I'm too pale." Her happiness grew when I modeled the green lawn.

I laughed as I undid the buttons. "I feel like a little girl playing in her mother's closet."

"Since you don't have the appropriate luggage to hold the outfits, store them in my trunk. Anytime you want to wear one, it's yours. For that matter, if you see another dress you might like to wear, help yourself."

I changed back into my brown calico and reluctantly returned the gowns to the trunk. My hand lingered on the smooth silk sleeve of the russet gown. I'd never owned such an elegant garment in my entire life and wasn't sure I should accept such expensive gifts from a stranger. As I tucked the bedcovers around Mary's neck, I thanked her again.

While she slept, I considered her request. She'd already insisted on paying for my ticket once she heard my story about Emmett. Now that I no longer owed Cy for the cost of my ticket, if I agreed to go with Mary, I could pay my own way to California and have a stake toward my trip to China. And Pa's twenty-dollar gold piece in the bottom of my sack—if I took the job, I could send it back to him immediately. However, I didn't like the thought of Joe and Cy continuing on toward San

Francisco without me.

I needed advice, not from Joe or even from Bertha, but from the God Bertha worshiped. I wanted to believe that Someone out there cared for me as much as the wise farm wife claimed He did. I longed to have the woman's faith. But all I could see whenever I closed my eyes was that stolen gold coin. *Can God forgive me? Will He forgive me? Does He even care? Do I have the right to ask?*

Every few hours, Bertha brought the infant to Mary to nurse. The child's best efforts ended in frustrated wails. Bertha did manage to get a few ounces of cow's milk into the baby by fashioning a container and nipple out of one of Mary's white kid gloves.

Periodically, the conductor checked to see how we were faring. On one of his visits he brought a telegram from Mary's husband in Kansas, saying he would meet her train in Kansas City, Missouri. As I listened to the conductor read the terse message, I knew that neither Mary nor the baby would survive traveling that distance alone.

Then I remembered Auntie Gert's advice, "God expects us to take only one step at a time." *Step one. What is step one? A wet nurse. The first step is a wet nurse for the baby.*

I stood, straightened my back, and gathered my courage. "Sir, how would I go about hiring a wet nurse for Mrs. McCall?"

He thought a moment, then broke into the first smile I'd seen on his face the entire trip. "The Hull House— Jane Addams's Hull House. I read about her place in the newspaper." He hurried to explain. "During the last ten years, hundreds of penniless European immigrants have arrived in Chicago. Miss Addams has set up a place where they can get help. If anyone can find a wet nurse for the little tyke, Miss Jane Addams can."

"Would I have time to get Mrs. McCall settled somewhere and locate a wet nurse before this train pulls out for San Francisco?"

"That won't be a problem, miss." He acted delighted to deliver a piece of good news. "Chicago is a seven-hour layover." Then he excused himself, leaving me alone in the semidarkened room.

That would solve my problem. A wet nurse could travel with Mary and the children to Kansas while I went on to California with Joe and Cy. I gazed at the sleeping woman. Probably in her late twenties, Mary had a delicate face. Blue veins stood out against the ghastly white of her forehead. The hand-embroidered lace of the cambric nightgown accented the woman's porcelain features. When I hung her beige traveling dress in the trunk, I read the label at the back, "Lady Fontabella Creations, imported silk shantung," a fabric I'd only read about in *Godey's Lady's Book.*

As the first rays of sunlight swept across the rolling landscape, I curled up on the floor beside the berth and fell asleep. Bertha found me in that position when she brought the baby for another attempt at feeding. "Chloe, why don't you let me take over while you get a few hours' sleep? The boys are taking care of Jamie. It's the least I can do before I leave you in Chicago."

I nodded and padded to my own bed. It wasn't until I awakened two hours later that I remembered Bertha's message. Of course she would change trains in Chicago to head toward Milwaukee, Wisconsin. *Thank God for Cy and Joe!*

Chicago Station

By the time the train pulled into Chicago, I had bathed and returned to Mary's compartment to discuss the financial arrangements she wished me to make with the wet nurse. Her eyes filled with tears as I explained my plan to turn her over to another. She insisted I wear the green lawn frock. "You must look the part of a wealthy lady procuring the services of a wet nurse."

I slipped into the dress and allowed her to button the tiny pearl buttons up the back. She insisted I wear the matching hat of lawn and netting that perched a little off center an inch or two above my forehead. I'd never before worn any head covering that didn't tie under the chin. Mary laughed as I pinned and fussed with the frothy confection until I was certain a gust of wind wouldn't dislodge it as I attempted to cross a busy intersection in the city.

"You look absolutely exquisite, Chloe! Don't forget the white ruffled parasol," Mary exclaimed. "Your Mr. Chamberlain will be enchanted."

Color flamed in my face. "*My* Mr. Chamberlain? Oh, no, you have it all wrong. He's hardly my Mr. Chamberlain."

Her eyes twinkled. A coy grin teased the corners of

her mouth upward. "Oh, really? I've seen the way he looks at you."

I shook my head, but she grinned knowingly. "You'll find a white linen purse and a pair of the white linen gloves in the top drawer of the trunk."

After assuring her that Bertha would be close by should she need assistance and that I'd take Jamie with me, I left the compartment.

Cy was talking with the cook in the dining section. "I'm ready, Cy. Where's Joe?"

Cy glanced over his shoulder at me; then whipped about, his mouth open.

"Is something wrong?" I inquired.

"Uh, no, uh . . . you look beautiful, Miss Chloe."

"Thank you. Where's Joe?"

Cy glanced down at the bowler hat in his hands. "Joe took Jamie to see the horses. He thought it might be better if Jamie stayed here with him while you and I go to Hull House."

That made sense. Dragging an upset child around a busy city like Chicago didn't seem appealing. Cy continued, "My parents and I visited the 1893 World's Columbian Exposition, so I am familiar with the city."

Alone with him? My mouth dried out. Determined not to appear like the farm girl I knew I was, I swallowed hard. "How very nice of you, Mr. Chamberlain."

He took my hand and placed it in the crook of his arm. "Then let's go, shall we?"

I felt like high-born royalty as Cy helped me from the train and over to the depot. We took a local train to the Randolph Street Station, then switched to the Blue Island Avenue streetcar. In detail, Cy explained how a streetcar worked, since I'd never seen one, let alone ridden on one before.

I leaned out of the streetcar to see the tops of the

monstrous red-brick buildings rising on each side of the street. Cy said they were called skyscrapers. The name seemed appropriate. People filled the wooden sidewalks in front of dingy shops and spilled out into the cobblestone streets.

"Before the exposition, no one took Chicago seriously. Easterners considered it to be nothing more than a dusty cow town. But, now, I can't believe the changes since I was here last." The bell clanged as we pulled away from a crowded curb. "The exposition had everything from an electric building to Venetian canals and gondolas. The planners imported dancing girls all the way from Cairo, Egypt. One newsman reported that the dancing girls were as homely as owls, but had voluptuous feet."

Cy told about riding on a 250-foot-high Ferris wheel, where each car held sixty people. When I admitted that I had no idea what a Ferris wheel looked like, he patiently described the contraption. He continued spewing forth information on the "windy city," as he called it. "Do you know Chicago even has its own baseball team? The Chicago White Stockings. They're not bad either."

At least I understood the game my brothers played with the other boys at school and the men played at the Fourth of July picnic. We got off the streetcar and walked the few blocks to Halsted Street. Halsted Street was a community of its own, a community of butcher shops, grocers, saloons, barber shops, and dry goods stores. Here, too, the streets were clogged with people, all speaking different languages. I remembered Pa reading from the Bible about the Tower of Babel and wondered if the people of the tower had all migrated to this busy midwestern avenue.

My palms perspired inside the white linen gloves as we entered the massive front door of the three-story

Hull House. A smiling young woman in a blue striped blouse and navy skirt met us in the hallway. When I asked to speak with Miss Addams, I learned she was at city hall, discussing with the mayor the lack of garbage pickup in the neighborhood.

The woman took in the expensive lawn dress I wore. "My name is Miss Beale. Perhaps I can help you. I'm Miss Addams's assistant."

Nervously, I smoothed imaginary wrinkles from the skirt of my gown as I explained my mission. Even to my ears, the story sounded too fantastic to believe. When I finished, the woman frowned. "That's a tall order—a mother who is nursing and is also willing to travel to Kansas with total strangers on such short notice. I don't know." Miss Beale asked a young boy of about ten years old, whom she called Eddie, to give us a tour of the establishment while she worked on our problem.

As Cy and I followed Eddie from room to room, I couldn't believe what I saw. In one area women looked after babies and young children so that their mothers could work in the local factories. A gym was filled with teenage boys playing games. Classrooms contained immigrants learning to speak English and women learning to cook and sew.

Cy and I exchanged glances—we were both impressed. Eddie returned us to the empty front parlor. Cy shook his head. "Really the place, isn't it? Every city should have a Hull House." He made himself comfortable on the faded gold brocade sofa to await Miss Beale's return.

Restless, I walked over to the library table by the windows and picked up a newspaper. The headlines told of the invasion of Cuba. Riley! Was my brother alive or dead? I hadn't thought about him in several days. I read in the news story of the carnage and felt selfish for causing my mother and father additional worry at such a time.

When Miss Beale entered the parlor, Cy and I stood. Her face broke into a wide smile. "I have a possible candidate for you. She is a young Polish woman named Else Beck. Else's husband died in an industrial accident last spring."

"And . . ." Cy urged impatiently.

Miss Beale continued, "A few weeks ago, Else gave birth to a stillborn. And since then, she's been supporting herself by hiring out as a wet nurse for a wealthy patron of Hull House. But for some reason, she was dismissed and needs employment."

"Wonderful." I clasped my hands together and cautiously touched my fingertips to my lips. "Is she available? Mrs. McCall is willing to cover all her expenses, including a round-trip ticket to Chicago, if the woman so desires."

Miss Beale shrugged. "I think Else's only relative in America is a married sister living in Denver, Colorado. Who knows? Perhaps Else can solve her problems while helping solve yours."

The woman scribbled a name and an address on a piece of paper. Blowing on it to dry the ink, she explained, "This is the name of a reputable boardinghouse near the depot. I would suggest you tell Mrs. McCall to wait there with her children until I've had a chance to talk with Mrs. Beck."

Hopes of being on board my brother and Cy's train for San Francisco faded. "When? How soon will I hear from you?"

"Tomorrow . . . the day after." She shrugged. "It's the best I can do."

Out of the corner of my eye I could see Cy bristle and draw himself up into the arrogant Chamberlain stance.

"Really, Miss Beale, Miss Spencer needs more information—"

"Thank you, Miss Beale." I grabbed his arm and urged him toward the front door. "I know you understand our need and will do everything humanly possible to help us."

Out on the street, Cy growled, "What was that all about? I could have made the woman—" His lips tightened into a grim line.

"She did all she could on such short notice. Besides, I need her on my side."

Cy's good humor didn't return until we reached the streetcar stop. The silence gave me time to consider my next step—move Mary and family to the boarding-house, then stay with them until the wet nurse arrived. Only then could I continue on to California.

Once I knew my mind, I relaxed and enjoyed the excitement of the big city. On the ride back to the depot I badgered Cy for information on every sight we passed. However, he never again matched my enthusiasm. The more excited I became, the more subdued he grew. He acted suspiciously like my father did before delivering one of his lectures.

"Chloe, don't get your hopes up. You may just have to leave Mary to solve her own problems. You don't know this Else character will take the job. What will you do then?"

When I hesitated, he eyed me suspiciously. "Bad question, huh? You aren't going to do what I think you're going to do, are you?"

"Well, not exactly."

His eyes narrowed. "What do you mean, not exactly?"

"I mean, I'm not sure. I can't abandoned the woman and her two children. Her health is delicate right now. And, frankly, the baby isn't doing well either."

"You aren't thinking of going to Kansas with her, are you?"

"Oh, no! No. I just figured I'd get Mary and the children settled in a boardinghouse and stay with her for a few days until I find someone to help her."

He shook his head and frowned. "That won't work. I'm sorry, but I can't stay in Chicago even one day longer. I have an important business engagement in San Francisco with some men from—"

My eyes met his. "I don't expect you to stay. After I get Mary situated, I'll come through later on another train."

"What?" He acted horrified at the suggestion. "A young girl like you traveling alone?"

I giggled into the back of my hand.

"All right, stupid response. You've been traveling alone, but now, now that you have your brother's protection."

"I know. Joe's going to be a problem. He can be as stubborn as my father."

Cy took my hand and with one finger, he drew spirals on the back of my gloved hand. "You know you will be all alone. You won't have anyone. Even Mrs. Schnetzler will be gone."

"I know." I bit my lip again. "It's all so insane. Forty-eight hours ago, I didn't even know Mary McCall and her children." Gently, I removed my hand from his. I tucked my arms about my waist as if warding off a frigid north wind. "Hey, it's a temporary detour. I'll be passing through California for China before you know it."

"China?"

I laughed and told him about the day the missionaries came to town.

"You are one incredible lady, Miss Chloe Spencer.

And you're everything my brother said you were—and more."

At the mention of Phillip, my face reddened. "He talked about me?"

"Oh, did he ever!" Cy nodded wryly. "You rekindled his fire to become a preacher, you know. My parents would never forgive you for that, if they knew. They'd prefer he be a rogue like me."

"You're not nearly as bad as you want people to think, Mr. Chamberlain."

"No, that's where you're wrong," he warned. "Frankly, I'm the opposite of my brother. I seldom think of anyone but myself."

I started to protest, but he touched his finger to my lips. "You were very wise not to trust me when I offered to have you travel with Joe and me. Remember, your first instincts are usually most accurate."

Our arrival at the main depot ended our strange conversation. Reluctantly, Cy stood and drew me to my feet. We faced one another half a second longer than necessary. Then he cleared his throat, breaking the spell. Resuming his role as the perfect gentleman, Cy helped me step down onto the cobblestone street.

Placing my hand in his arm, he hurried me through the station to the platform. A crowd of curious travelers had gathered around the company Pullman, which was being restocked with supplies. "I can't believe I'm being so honest. Woman, you are dangerous. Maybe I should be glad you're staying here a few days, giving me time to get my shady ethics back on track."

I searched his face, trying to determine whether he was serious. "Just joking."

Bertha waved to us from an open window on the private car. Cy took my elbow and propelled me forward. "We'd better hurry if we intend to get you and the

McCalls settled at the boardinghouse before the train pulls out."

After helping me into the railway car, Cy turned to speak with the conductor, and I hurried into the parlor, where Bertha sat. The new baby slept on the sofa surrounded by pillows, while Jamie sat at her feet, playing with a stack of travel brochures.

I unpinned the hat and tossed it onto the stand beside the sofa. "How is everyone?"

Jamie looked up and smiled. Bertha grinned.

"Where's Joe?"

"He went to check on the horses a few minutes ago."

I took off my gloves. "We hurried as fast as we could. How are Mary and the baby doing?"

"Mary slept most of the time you were gone, as has the baby," Bertha reported. "And this little guy should fall asleep soon, I would think. Did you find someone?" She motioned for me to sit down beside her.

I sucked in my breath, knowing she wouldn't like my answer. "I'm not sure. It's not certain, but there's this young widow who might be interested in a free trip to Denver."

"Good. So why am I detecting worry in your face?"

Gazing at the trains being serviced on the different tracks, I explained about the boardinghouse and having to stay behind for a few days. "I don't know what God wants me to do. I wish He would just write on the wall or on tables of stone like in Bible times."

Bertha eyed me for a few seconds before speaking. "Chloe, God isn't a wealthy grandpa who supplies easy answers and grants your every wish, you know. He knows the beginning from the end, and He does promise to guide you if you wait on Him for the answers. Would you like to pray about it?"

Startled, I glanced around as if the room were full of

people who might overhear us. Without a word, Bertha dropped to her knees. She waited as I did the same. Jamie continued to scatter the leaflets about the floor of the car.

Taking my hands in hers, she said, "Heavenly Father, You are the all-wise and all-knowing God. Your Word says, 'If any of you lack wisdom, let him ask of God.'" She paused and squeezed my fingers. "Well, we're asking. We need a generous portion of Your wisdom. At least four people's futures depend on Your keeping Your promises."

She continued, praying for each of us individually— Mary, Jamie, the baby, Else, and last, me. I'd never heard anyone actually pray for me before. "Father, I believe every promise You ever made. But Chloe here, well, she's not seen the marvelous things You can do for Your children. Guide her during the next few hours as she decides what she must do. Amen."

Bertha squeezed my fingers again and whispered, "It's your turn."

I gulped. I'd never prayed in front of anyone before. I wasn't even sure that the praying I'd done was really praying. Haltingly, I began. "Dear God, I'm not too good at this. But I need Your help right now." Pa's twenty-dollar gold piece flashed before my eyes. I swallowed hard. "I've done some pretty stupid things in the last few days. I want You to know that I am sorry. If I could do everything over . . . Please don't hold my sins against Mary and her children."

I choked out an amen and scrambled to my feet. My eyes brimmed with tears. I walked to the end of the car and stared into the observation lounge. Bertha came up behind me and put her arm around my shoulders. "Don't worry, child. Our God is in the business of forgiving sins."

As I dabbed my tears on the sleeve of my dress, Joe burst into the lounge. "What's going on? Cy says you have some crazy idea of staying in Chicago for a few days. He's out somewhere right now, trying to rent a room for the four of you."

I turned slowly and placed my hand on his arm. "Joe, please try to understand. Mary and the baby need someone. So does little Jamie."

"Well, that someone doesn't have to be you!"

"Then who?"

He loomed over me like a menacing thundercloud. His eyebrows knitted into one solid glare. "Not you!"

"What do you think Pa would do if he were me?" I lifted one eyebrow and waited for him to answer. He stared into my eyes for several seconds without responding. "Sorry, Joe, but you just helped me make my decision. I'm staying with Mary and the baby until they are safely on their way to Kansas."

He ran his fingers through his short-cropped brown hair. "I don't get it, Chloe. Why are you all of a sudden becoming responsible? You're the one who always turned tail and ran when something needed doing on the farm."

I started to protest. He interrupted. "Hey, do you think none of us knew what you were doing, hiding up there in Pa's herb loft? So why become responsible now?"

I raised my hands in defense. "Sorry. It's just something I have to do. As I said, Pa—"

"Speaking of Pa, I sent a third telegram. I can't imagine what's happening back there."

I stared down at the floor. "I'm sorry." I jumped when Bertha touched my arm. I'd forgotten she was still there.

"You're sure this is what you want to do?"

"As sure as I can be, unless God tells me to do

something else." My eyes begged her to understand. "Last night you said God placed you here on this train for a purpose. Well, maybe this is my purpose for being here."

My brother swung about to face me. "That's ridiculous! You used bad judgment and ran away from home. You just happened to be on this train when the woman went into labor. By accident, Chloe, not by design."

I didn't know how to respond to his unaccustomed vehemence. "Joe, whether it was bad judgment or accident or design that brought me into this situation is immaterial. I'm here now. I can't turn and walk away from what I believe is my God-given responsibility."

Joe stormed from the lounge. As the door slammed, Jamie curled up into a little ball and buried his head in his arms. I wrapped my arms about my waist and shuddered. Of all the people I needed on my side, it was my brother. I felt horribly alone and empty.

Bertha gathered me into her arms and held me for a moment. "Don't be afraid, dear. If you really believe this is God's will for you, you'll be fine, no matter how big the problem."

"I hope so."

Mr. Schnetzler tapped on the window and pointed toward the train next to us. "Bertha, we've got to go," he mouthed.

She flung her arms in the air. "I wish I could be here for you, child, but—I'm terribly sorry." She stepped back. Her work-hardened hands lingered on mine. "I'm sorry."

"I understand, and don't worry, I'll be fine." I kissed her on the cheek. "I'll never forget you, you know."

Bertha kissed the sleeping infant on the forehead, then did the same with Jamie. I gathered the baby into my arms, and with Jamie close at my heels, I followed

Bertha down the corridor toward the exit. As we passed the sleeping compartments, she took one last peek at Mary. At the steps, Bertha kissed me again. "Remember, I'll be praying for you."

I watched her walk away from the coach. My head and neck ached. *What am I doing? I shouldn't have to make decisions like this! I'm just a kid. Oh, Pa, if only you were here.*

"But he's not here! Nobody's here—except you and me, kiddo!" I announced to Jamie and to tiny Agatha Melvina. The bundle in my arms whimpered.

"Such a long name for such a little body," I cooed. "Maybe I'll call you Vini." I glanced down at Jamie. He looked up and smiled.

"So now, Jamie boy, where do we go from here?" By the moistness seeping through the baby's lightweight blanket I knew what my next step would be. I took a deep breath and pasted a smile on my face. "One step at a time."

I hurried into my compartment and changed the baby. Rather than disturb Mary, I decided to use Bertha's makeshift bottle to feed the baby. When the glove became saturated, the butler had attached a kid glove to a pint-sized milk bottle from the kitchen. The butler filled the bottle with diluted cow's milk and warmed it.

The little boy with the dark, somber eyes stared at me, his face solemn and unreadable. I listened as the infant slurped at the milk. Even through the blankets I could feel a strange gurgle or wheeze in her chest that worried me. I placed the baby on the berth and surrounded her with pillows, then rushed about, repacking Mary's trunk and preparing to deboard the train. When Mary wakened, I told her everything that had happened and the plans I'd made thus far. Every few minutes, I checked out the window, hoping to see either

Cy pull up outside with a rented team and carriage or the wet nurse arrive. Still in the back of my mind, I hoped the nurse would arrive in time to allow me to continue on to California with Cy and Joe.

Thirty minutes before the train was to leave for California, a rented carriage pulled up beside the Pullman. The coach and the stable car were already on line when Cy leaped from the carriage and bounded into the coach. The conductor and Joe followed closely behind.

Joe took Jamie into his arms while the conductor ordered the baggage men to haul Mary's luggage over to the carriage. Cy took hold of my arm, his eyes brimming with concern. "Everything's arranged for you at the boardinghouse. I rented a carriage and went back to Hull House. Mrs. Beck has agreed to go to Kansas with the understanding that Mary pay her expenses and buy her a ticket on to Denver when the time comes."

A new wave of tears surfaced, tears of gratitude. "Oh, thank you, Cy. You've been such a big help."

Brushing my gratitude aside, he continued. "I sent a telegram to Mr. McCall to confirm that he will meet the train in Kansas City, Missouri. I reserved first-class sleeper compartments for all of you. If for some reason you cannot leave by then, notify the ticket agent."

Relief flooded through me. Only the thought of my mother's horror kept me from planting a thank-you kiss on the grinning young man's cheek. "I-I-I don't know what to say. Thank you doesn't seem like enough."

Cy beamed with pleasure. "Don't say anything. I've had more fun in the last two days than I did the time my parents lost me in Paris, France, for twelve whole hours! Thank *you*."

Joe stood with his back turned. "Please, Joe. I need your blessing. It won't be long, and I'll join you in California—probably in less than two weeks."

He set Jamie down beside me. "Come on, Cy, we'd better help Mary. You can handle Jamie and the baby, can't you, Chloe?"

"Of course."

After settling Mary and the children in the carriage, Cy gave the driver directions to the boardinghouse. Joe stood on the opposite side of the carriage next to where Jamie sat clutching his mother's arm while Cy walked over to where I stood. "Chloe, I'm sorry I can't help you further. I feel like I'm abandoning you."

"No, you've done more than enough." I glanced at my brother, then back at Cy. "You're a good friend. Thank you for everything."

"You have the name of the hotel in San Francisco where we'll be staying, don't you?" His face filled with concern. "I'll be seeing you in California before the end of July, right?"

I lifted one eyebrow and smiled. "I'm certainly going to try."

I'm sure his mother would have been as shocked as mine when he leaned over and kissed my cheek. "Do more than try."

I watched as he strode toward the Pullman coach. When I turned to climb into the waiting carriage, Joe came over and kissed my other cheek. " 'Bye, Chloe Mae."

Sniffing back my tears, I kissed him, then with his help, climbed into the carriage. The driver urged the horses forward. I leaned out the side of the carriage and waved until we rounded the first corner.

The world of steam engines, steel rails, and railroad yards immediately shifted to one of clanging streetcars, clopping horses, and the energetic bustle of the city. Within minutes the carriage eased to a stop in front of a three-story boardinghouse. I asked the driver how much I owed him.

"The gentleman already covered the fees, ma'am, for today and for the trip to the depot on Friday morning at 8:30 a.m."

A woman with black hair bustled from the house and introduced herself as Mrs. DeMarko. The carriage driver carried Mary's luggage into the boardinghouse and up the steps to the rooms Cy had reserved for us. Jamie followed behind as Mrs. DeMarko and I helped Mary up to the room. When I asked how much the rooms would cost, the landlady waved me away. "The gentleman took care of everything, miss."

The landlady helped Jamie haul his mother's large satchel up the steps while I lined an empty bureau drawer with a light quilt and placed the sleeping infant inside. After requesting that Mrs. DeMarko send for a doctor, I attended to Mary. The darkened areas under her eyes and her pale, sunken cheeks worried me. I fought against the possibility that she might not survive.

When I suggested he take a nap, Jamie willingly crawled into the big feather bed in the room next door to his mother's. I stayed with him until he fell asleep. Then I went to see Mary. The moment I stepped inside her room, I heard the baby's raspy wheeze. I walked over to the bureau and felt the infant's forehead. It seemed a little too warm.

Anxiety creased Mary's brow. "What's the matter? What's wrong with my baby?"

I cleared my throat. "I'm not sure, but I'll have the doctor check her too. When I go to bed tonight, I'll take her in with me, drawer and all, so that you can get a good night's sleep. In the meantime, what can I do for you?"

"I know you're busy and very tired, but . . ." She looked embarrassed. "Would you mind reading to me for a few minutes?"

Mary watched as I retrieved the Bible from her case. "Could you read Psalm 23?"

I located the chapter and began to read. "The Lord is my shepherd; I shall not want. He maketh me . . ." I read the words aloud as if hearing them for the first time. My mother had always claimed that this psalm brought her such comfort, especially after she left her parents' home for northern Pennsylvania. As I read, I thought about the loneliness she must have felt, stranded in a strange place, fifteen years old and expecting her first child.

I read on. "Yea, though I walk through the valley of the shadow of death . . ." I glanced toward Mary. She'd drifted off to sleep. I laid the book on the table beside the bed, adjusted her covers, and tiptoed from the room.

Kansas Ho

Soon after the mahogany grandfather clock at the foot of the stairs gonged four, the doorbell rang. From the top of the stairs, I watched Mrs. DeMarko rush to answer the door. A tall, weathered old man stepped inside the house. When the woman greeted him and invited him to follow her upstairs, I slipped back inside Mary's room and waited for Mrs. DeMarko's knock.

"Chloe, Doc Haynes is here to examine Mrs. McCall and the newborn."

I opened the door. One look in the man's eyes, and I felt like a nine-year-old schoolgirl caught cheating on a spelling test. The towering gentleman glared down at me over the silver rim of his spectacles. With merely a grunt, he brushed past me. I stayed frozen in place until I heard the door close. Mrs. DeMarko gave a brisk nod and hurried down the stairs to her living quarters.

I'd never met a genuine medical doctor. Butterflies fluttered against the walls of my stomach as I made my way to a small sun room at the end of the hallway. Nervously I watched the minute hand on a rosewood mantel clock inch forward.

Fifteen minutes later he opened the door and walked down the hall toward me, holding the baby in his arms. "So you're the little gal who brought this beautiful lady into the world?" He placed the baby in my arms. The infant stuffed her fist into her mouth and sucked.

"Yes, sir."

He chuckled deep into the wrinkled folds of his throat. "Well, you did a mighty fine job. I could use someone like you. How old are you anyway, fourteen?"

I sighed with relief. "I'll be seventeen in August."

"I'm serious about the job offer. With all the immigrants flowing into the city, I don't even have time to clean my spectacles."

"Thank you for your kind offer, but I'm heading for California. My brother Joe will be waiting."

"Ah, California!" he snorted. "Can't see it myself. There's something unnatural about living with all that sunshine! If you should change your mind . . ."

I smiled and patted the baby nervously. "And, Mary, er, Mrs. McCall? Is she going to be all right?"

He shook his head and sighed. "Women have been having babies since the beginning of time, yet we know so little about the process. Frankly, I'm more concerned about the child." His gaze darkened. "Her lungs don't sound good, probably not fully developed. And she's a might small."

"Well, she did come earlier than the Creator intended," I reminded.

He nodded and cleared his throat. "Watch her carefully. If the child makes it through the next forty-eight hours, she'll probably live to produce healthy babies of her own someday. I left a bottle of spring tonic to help Mrs. McCall regain her strength."

"Dr. Haynes, I feel so terrible. What did I do wrong?"

He wagged his finger in my face. "Absolutely nothing! Don't imagine blame where there is none. Believe me, this old fussbudget wouldn't try to lure you away from that California gold if you'd done a careless job with Mrs. McCall or the baby."

"Oh, I don't know. What if . . ."

"Listen, Missy, I believe in placing blame where blame is due. And as far as little Agatha Melvina's health is concerned, only the good Lord knows the reasons."

I listened as he prescribed the proper dosage of the tonic he'd left, then asked, "Would it help Mary or the child to remain here in Chicago a little longer?"

He peered at me over his spectacles. "Undoubtedly. However, Mrs. McCall seems mighty determined to go on to Kansas."

"There must be something . . ."

"All I can tell you is, keep doing what you're doing."

I handed the doctor the money Mary had given me for his visit and watched him descend the stairs. When he'd gone, I closed my eyes. "Please, heavenly Father. I can't do this alone; please help me."

I jumped at the sound of Mrs. DeMarko calling to me from the foot of the stairs. "Miss Spencer, a Mrs. Beck has arrived. Shall I send her up?"

An answer to my prayer so quickly? I clapped my hands and whispered a hasty Thank You, then skipped down the stairs. Standing next to Mrs. DeMarko in the boardinghouse entryway was a woman with sandy blond hair who appeared to be in her early twenties. Mrs. Beck's delicate face appeared pinched and anxious. The gaze from her watery blue eyes darted nervously toward our landlady, then to the floor. I extended my hand as I approached. "You are a welcome sight, Mrs. Beck."

The wet nurse set her case on the Oriental carpet and brought a thin, birdlike hand up to meet mine. I smiled and captured her hand between my two. "You do speak English, don't you?"

Mrs. Beck grinned weakly. "A little."

"Good. That's a start. We'll work out the rest as we go." I put my arm about the woman's shoulders and led her upstairs. Mrs. DeMarko followed with the valise. "Do you have a trunk as well?"

"No, ma'am. This is it."

"Fine. Please call me Chloe. First, you need to meet Mrs. McCall and her son, Jamie." I opened the door to Mary's room. Else followed me inside. After introducing the two women, I left them alone to get acquainted.

Out in the hallway, the middle-aged Mrs. DeMarko waited, her arms folded across her expansive waist. "I don't trust the woman. You watch your step with her."

"I beg your pardon?"

Her eyes narrowed. "Mark my word. She's not everything she pretends to be. Be careful around her."

"Mrs. DeMarko, I hardly think . . ."

She silenced me. "You are too gullible and too honest. Just be careful."

Honest? Pa's twenty-dollar gold piece. I felt a wave of heat suffusing my neck and face. "Th-th-thank you, Mrs. DeMarko, for the warning. I'll be careful."

Lifting her chin in satisfaction, the woman gathered her skirt and marched downstairs. The massive bun perched atop her head bobbed rhythmically with each determined step. I returned to the room to find Mary longingly watching as Else nursed the ravenous baby. Jamie wandered into the room behind me and over to his mother. At her insistence, Mary dictated while I wrote out an agreement of payment for the two women to sign. Satisfied with the provisions, the nurse signed the document. Mary's hand shook as she scribbled her signature on the delicately scented writing paper.

I took the fountain pen from her hands and returned it to the crystal inkwell on the bureau. "Now you need to rest," I suggested.

Mary turned her head from side to side. "No. Please fetch a second piece of writing paper and write out another agreement, this time between you and me. I trust you, Chloe."

I winced at the mention of the word *trust*.

She paused and frowned. "I must be certain that you will stick by Jamie and the baby, especially if—if something happens to me."

"Nothing's going to—"

She raised her hand to silence me. "Please, I am sorry to pressure you about this, but my children . . . I must make provision for the safety of my children."

"I'll do anything I can." My heart sank. *Will I ever reach California?* I dipped the pen in the inkwell and prepared to record her wishes.

The way Else's eyes darted from my face to Mary's as I wrote, I knew the nurse understood more English than she spoke. After signing the agreement, Mary sighed and glanced over at her daughter resting in the other woman's arms. "I would like to talk with you alone, Chloe," Mary whispered.

I smiled at Mrs. Beck. "Would you please take the baby next door into my room and change her diaper?"

The door closed behind the woman before Mary continued. "Chloe, there is a fake bottom in my portmanteau. Beneath it you will find a small box of jewelry. If anything happens, see that James's Aunt Beatrice receives the emerald brooch." I scribbled down the instructions for the distribution of rings, necklaces, and other precious items. "Also, I want you to give Mrs. Beck two of the silver dollars in my velvet pouch so she won't feel restricted during the trip. You take two also."

"That's not necess—"

She raised her hand to stop my protest. "I think I'll

rest for a while."

After retrieving the coins from her travel case, I took Jamie's hand and hurried to my room. Mrs. Beck wasn't there. We found her and the baby in her own room. I gave her two of the coins and slipped the other two into my skirt pocket. "Why don't you bring Baby Vini down to the sun room so you and I can get acquainted?"

Together we strolled down the hall and into the sunny parlor. The nurse chose to sit in a painted wicker rocker while I sat at one end of a chaise lounge upholstered in yellow-checked chintz. Jamie scrambled into the chair behind me and peered around my shoulder at Mrs. Beck. Try as I might, I could not convince him to make friends with the woman. If I'd had any doubt about detouring with Mary to Kansas, the fear in his big brown eyes convinced me I'd made the right choice.

The nurse and I talked for some time. I answered her questions about Mary and how I'd met her. Then I asked a few questions of my own. The nurse sniffed back her tears as she told me about her titled Polish parents and her German husband. "They disinherited me when I married Oscar and moved to America. It was so terrible; I'd never been poor before in my life."

Else's story made me realize how disappointed my parents must be in me. Obviously, while running away had rid me of Emmett, I'd only traded one set of problems for others. I decided that as soon as I reached California, I'd write a letter begging their forgiveness.

I wanted to say something comforting to Else and remembered Bertha's words about letting God work out our problems. But memory of the past week clamped my lips shut. *Who am I to give advice on problem solving?*

"If only I could go home to Poland," she sniffed.

Our conversation ceased when Mrs. DeMarko called

us downstairs to dinner.

Mrs. DeMarko and I spent part of the next day washing diapers and Jamie's clothes, preparing for the trip to Kansas. Jamie stayed close to me, occupying himself with the clothespins from the laundry basket.

When Jamie fell asleep on the floor, Mrs. DeMarko carried him into the parlor and laid him on the sofa, then returned. "He never talks or laughs. It's so sad."

I placed the cold iron on the stove and picked up a heated one. "Yes, I've wondered if he's mentally impaired."

She chuckled and shook her head. "There's nothing wrong with that child's brain. Don't be misled. He understands everything you and I say."

"Then I don't understand. Why doesn't he speak or cry or laugh—something?" I shoved the iron across the cotton fabric of one of Jamie's shirts.

"My guess is he's angry or frightened about something. I expect he'll come out of it in time. Be patient."

Sweat poured from me as I pressed the wrinkles out of the child's shirts and dungarees. I'd always hated ironing dungarees. Else entered the kitchen, asking for a glass of cool lemonade. Irked that the woman did nothing to help, Mrs. DeMarko suggested that Else help us. The wet nurse looked pleadingly at me. "The heavy labor might upset my nursing the baby."

Concerned that any work might lessen the woman's milk supply, I encouraged Else to go to her room and rest while I finished the ironing. Else smiled gratefully, poured herself a glass of water, and went back upstairs to her room.

"Never heard of such a thing!" Mrs. DeMarko huffed about the kitchen.

After finishing the washing and ironing, Mrs. DeMarko made a bed for little Vini out of a shopping basket she found in her attic. She lined the basket with flannel and blue gingham.

By Thursday evening, Mary's trunks were packed with newly laundered clothes. A giant stack of sunshine-fresh diapers sat on the floor beside the bed. After taking a cool sponge bath, I fell onto the bed, exhausted, but delighted with my accomplishments.

The next morning, the carriage arrived to take us to the station. A moist, oppressing heat danced off the cobblestones. The driver and his helper loaded the trunks onto the vehicle while Mrs. DeMarko and I helped Mary down the stairs and into the carriage. Mrs. Beck followed with the children.

"You could stay a week or two longer, dear," Mrs. DeMarko urged. "It would give Mary time to get her strength back and the baby time to grow a little."

I smiled into her eager eyes. "You are—"

"No!" Startled, we turned to face Mary's determined glare. "No! I must go today."

I glanced at the two women and shrugged.

"Oh." Mrs. DeMarko's hand flew to her mouth. "I almost forgot. Don't go anywhere!" She disappeared into the house and returned carrying a red felt draw-string pouch. Bending down to meet Jamie eye to eye, she looped the strings around his wrist. "This is for you. Don't open it until you're on the train."

Mrs. Beck watched as Mary and I thanked the plain, generous woman for her kindness. "I'll say a novena for you, Chloe, dear," Mrs. DeMarko added. "You are a precious child."

After I checked that all the luggage had been loaded on board, I hugged Mrs. DeMarko goodbye. The driver helped us into the carriage. I tugged at my starched white collar and wished I'd worn something less constricting. As the carriage rolled toward the depot, my discomfort was replaced with a surge of excitement. I was on my way once more. *Kansas-ho!*

Steam hissed impatiently from beneath waiting trains, ready to depart for all points west—Kansas City, Denver, Santa Fe, Dallas, and, of course, San Francisco. My excitement intensified as I made my way through the travelers scurrying about the train station. It felt good to be among people who had places to go and things to do. I was eager to shed the lethargy that had built up during the previous days of waiting and worrying. We were on our way; everything was going to be all right.

After the ticket agent handed me our sheaf of tickets, I asked if there were any messages for me. I was hoping Pa had responded to my telegram. My day would be complete if I could only read his words, "You are forgiven."

The agent shook his head. Even though Joe had probably notified my parents of my detour, I decided to send another telegram explaining. In a minimum of words, I told my change in plans and promised to write.

The ticket agent arranged for a porter to assist Mary on board. "Else, you go with Mary and the baby. I'll be along in a minute." Else frowned, but did as she was told.

"Come on, Jamie, you come with me." His face distorted with fear, and he stretched out his hand toward his mother. "Mama's not going to leave without us, I promise. We're just going to get you something to play with on the train."

He gave me his silent stare, then took my hand. In the little shop next to the ticket booth, I let him choose six postcards, three brightly colored paintings of Chicago and the World's Columbian Exposition, and three sepia-toned photographs. After paying for the cards

from the money Mary had given me, I placed them in
the purse Mary had insisted I carry. I wove my way,
with Jamie in tow, across the crowded platform and
into the Pullman sleeper car where we'd been assigned.

The simple accommodations contrasted starkly to
the opulent display in Cy's private coach. *Oh, well, it's
better than the passenger day coach. A week ago you
would have thought this to be luxury!*

Else chose the berth next to Mary's, so I took the one
across the aisle. After depositing my personal belongings inside, I helped Mary settle in; then I made my way
to one of the dozen window seats at the front of the
coach.

Jamie scrambled up in the seat beside me and held
out his hand. "What do you want, Jamie?"

He pointed at the purse where I'd placed the postcards. "You'll have to tell me what you want." The
child's stony silence bothered me. Surely a boy of five
should be chattering like a flock of sparrows in spring.
He jabbed at my purse again. The stubborn glint in his
eyes told me he knew what I was trying to do.

"I need to know what you want."

He answered me with a silent glare. I marveled to
myself at how, in such a short time, the stubborn little
boy had attached himself to my heart.

Defeated, I unfastened the metal clasp and handed
him the cards. Satisfied, he settled back against the
seat, content to study the pictures. I watched the station master confer with the conductor, both comparing
their pocket watches with the big clock in the depot,
then winding them in unison. The water boy, with his
copper bucket and dipper, strode up to the train, waved
to the conductor, asked the time, and swung on board.

Suddenly we were moving. Friends waved at the
passengers as the locomotive chugged out of the station.

My pulse raced as the train picked up speed in the tenement neighborhoods of lower Chicago. *West, I'm heading west—well, a little southwest, but generally west.*

Large rambling homes with expansive lawns and picket fences quickly replaced the cityscape. I watched as the houses grew farther apart. Before long, the familiar fields of ripening corn stretched toward the horizon or toward clumps of trees shrouding the clapboard farmhouses. Occasionally we stopped in a village to pick up or deposit passengers; otherwise, we hurled through the tiny settlements, forcing wagons, horses, and pedestrians to watch the passing drama.

Mary slept much of the afternoon. The ride to the station had tired her more than either of us realized. After nursing Vini, Else deposited her and the basket with me, then strolled to the front of the train.

I didn't mind. After all, where was I going to go? What else did I have to do? I looked down at the sleeping infant, watching for a moment the ragged rise and fall of her chest. *Is it my imagination, or has her breathing worsened?* I studied the tiny body as she labored for each breath. *I don't like the looks of her. I don't like it at all.*

"Oh, dear God, I don't like this at all."

The water boy entered through the back door and made his way up the aisle. I considered stopping him to ask if there was a physician on board. Then I remembered Dr. Haynes. I'd almost forgotten his dire warning. Counting the hours since his visit, I prayed, "But, Father, she's almost made it through the forty-eight hours he predicted. A little longer. Help her to hold on a little longer. After all, there's nothing magical about forty-eight hours, is there?"

I patted the child's chest and whispered soothing

words. Jamie glanced down at the basket once, then returned his attention to the postcards. The romance of the day disappeared as I kept watch over the baby. At suppertime I found Else and suggested she care for the baby while I took Jamie to the dining car and arranged for a tray of food for Mary. Else tightened her lips but said nothing. When she reached down for the baby basket, I warned her to keep a close watch over the baby and to fetch me if there was a change.

After we ate, I helped ready Jamie for bed. He kissed his mother good night and climbed into my bunk, still clutching the postcards. I offered to put them in my purse, but he shook his head and rolled over to face the wall. After checking on Else and the baby, I turned my attention to Mary. I hoped she wouldn't ask about Vini.

"You seem to be stronger, now that we're traveling. Or is it the doctor's elixir?"

She chuckled aloud. "Just knowing I'll be seeing James soon is enough medicine for me."

"Regardless, don't stop the medicine." Without her asking, I picked up Mary's Bible from the foot of her bed. "What would you like me to read to you tonight?" She chose Revelation 21.

As I read from the book of Revelation, I became engrossed in the writer's description of the new earth. I'd read down to verse 19 when Mary whispered, "Please, Chloe, would you read the verse about no more tears once again?"

My eyes skimmed back to verse 4. "God shall wipe away all tears from their eyes; and there shall be no more death, neither sorrow, nor crying, neither shall there be any more pain: for the former things are passed away." I glanced over at a smiling Mary. Her eyes were closed. A tear trickled down her cheek.

"I wonder what it feels like to die. Chloe, are you ever

afraid of dying?"

"Dying? What an awful thought!"

"Well, are you?"

For a moment I saw my father bending over a neighbor who had just died of pneumonia. I shuddered. "I try not to think about it. And neither should you!"

"My twin sister, Martha, died when we were ten. She fell into the pond behind our house and drowned. I've always wondered what it was like."

I closed the Bible and laid it on the foot of her bed. "Why don't you rest awhile? Later, after Vini's finished nursing, I'll bring her in for you to hold."

I picked up the Bible, closed the curtains, and peeked in on Jamie. He hadn't moved a muscle. I whispered to Else that I needed a few minutes alone, then tiptoed down the aisle to the seating area at the front of the sleeper car. Finding all the seats occupied, I wandered into the dining car to an empty table and sat down. There I opened the Bible to where I'd left off reading. I finished the twenty-first chapter and read on. "And the leaves of the tree were for the healing of the nations."

Leaves for healing? The aroma of my father's herb loft flooded my senses—rosemary, thyme, peppermint. I closed the book and laid it on the white linen tablecloth. With my fingertip, I traced the outline of a dogwood blossom tooled into the brown leather cover. One decision, and all was changed. I felt totally alone and hopelessly lost. I leaned my head against the window and watched shadows rush past in the moonless night. *Will I ever see my Pennsylvania home again?*

The familiar rocking of the train soothed my troubled mind. I didn't bother to open my eyes when the train paused in a darkened Illinois town. I didn't stir until I felt someone shaking my shoulder. I stared up into the conductor's stoic face.

"Miss Spencer? Miss Spencer!"

"Huh? Oh, yes?" I shook the sleep from my body.

"Mrs. McCall is calling for you. I told her I'd find you."

"Thank you very much, sir. I'll go to her immediately." I hurried to the sleeper car. I heard Mary's screams before I entered the sleeper car. Anyone who had been sleeping earlier, wasn't now. Angry, questioning faces followed my progress down the aisle. *What is going on? Where is Else? Surely she's not sleeping through Mary's cries.*

Mary leaned against Else's berth, cradling Vini to her breast. Jamie's frightened dark eyes peered out from behind the curtain across the aisle. I tried to calm her, but she continued to wail.

"What is it? Mary, calm down and tell me what's the—" Suddenly I knew. "Mary, give me Agatha."

Mary turned to face me; her cries dissolving into whimpers. "Agatha isn't breathing, Chloe. Else killed my baby."

"No, no, Mary. Else didn't harm your child." The eyes of every traveler in the coach silently watched as I coaxed the still form from Mary's arms. "Mary, please get back into bed while I check your daughter."

"It's no use. It's too late. She killed my baby," Mary wailed again as she crawled into her own berth and turned to face the wall.

I placed the infant on Else's bed and pressed my ear against her chest. The silence confirmed what I'd suspected the moment I'd taken the child from her mother's arms. Where was Else? Slowly, I straightened and turned toward the nearest onlooker, a stocky, balding man wearing a calf-length nightshirt.

"Please, sir, get the conductor. I need a doctor, now!" His eyes bulged as he bobbed his head up and down like a spring toy, then pushed his way through the crowded aisle toward the dining car.

Aware that I could do no more for either Mary or Agatha at the moment, I remembered Jamie. I turned and found myself face to face with Jamie's dark, fear-filled eyes. At that moment a young woman with thick ebony hair pushed through the gawking crowd. "Can I help? Will the little boy come with me?"

I shrugged and looked back at the silent five-year-old. "Jamie, will you let this nice lady take you to the dining car for a cup of hot chocolate? She'll help you put on your clothes while I take care of your mama."

When he nodded, I kissed his forehead. "As soon as I get your mother feeling a little better, I'll come and get you, all right?" He nodded again and stared up into the face of the helpful stranger. The woman lifted him into her arms, reached for his clothing that I'd stacked at the foot of the berth, and disappeared through the crowd. I stared down at a line of blue embroidered ducks marching across Agatha's pink flannel blanket, wishing I could block out the moaning coming from Mary's berth.

A few minutes later the conductor arrived, flanked by two porters and an elderly man carrying a large black bag. The conductor introduced the man as Dr. Morrow. As I explained the events of the past week to the doctor, he removed a stethoscope from his bag, placed the metal piece on baby Agatha's chest, and listened. He repeated the action at three other points on the tiny body, then put away his equipment and shook his head.

Without glancing my direction, he turned to the conductor and issued a string of instructions. Wrapping the infant in the blanket, the doctor handed the body to the nearest porter, then turned to me.

"Where is the baby's mother?" Dr. Morrow asked.

"Mrs. McCall's in here." I pulled back the curtain. Mary lay rigidly on her spine, staring at the ceiling. The doctor glanced at her, then at the curious spectators.

"Will you people kindly return to your berths and give this poor woman some privacy?" The people disappeared in a flurry of embarrassment. The physician took Mary's limp hand in his and spoke to her gently.

When she didn't respond, he turned to me. "Perhaps you can answer a few questions for me."

"Has this woman been nursing the child?"

"No, but we hired a wet nurse in Chicago. The baby was born prematurely on the train between Cleveland and Chicago. Dr. Haynes, a doctor who checked the baby in Chicago, said the infant's lungs weren't fully developed." I rubbed my upper arms, warding off a sudden chill. "But I thought . . . Oh, I was certain she'd make it."

"And this wet nurse? Where is she now?"

I shook my head and stifled a yawn. "I'm sorry. I haven't seen Mrs. Beck since I put Jamie down for the night. The conductor is searching the train for her."

"Jamie?" The man questioned. "Who is Jamie?"

"Jamie is Mrs. McCall's five-year-old son."

"I see." The doctor tapped his stethoscope on the back of his hand and pondered my words.

When I failed to stifle a second yawn, I covered my mouth with my hand.

"You are one tired young lady, Miss Spencer. Since I'm not going anywhere until the train stops, I'll watch over Mrs. McCall while you get some sleep." He shook the end of the stethoscope at me. "And that's an order!"

"I don't think I can sleep after all that's happened."

"At least go to the dining car and get yourself a hot drink to help you relax."

And More Kansas

The train swayed rhythmically, the iron wheels clicking along the rails. I groped my way to the dining car, where Mary's Bible still sat on the table where I'd abandoned it. At the far end of the car, the raven-haired woman waved. I could see the back of Jamie's head. I started toward them, but she shook her head and waved me away.

Shrugging, I sat down at the table where I'd dined earlier. A porter instantly appeared at my side and took my order for a cup of mint tea and a slice of toast. When I tried to pick up the teacup, my hand shook, and I spilled the hot brew into the saucer. Inside, my brain felt equally unstable. I opened the Bible and tried to read, but the words swam before my eyes. Peering out the window into the darkness, I saw a familiar face, my mother's, instead of my own. Trails of wrinkles fanned out from the dark smudges that underscored my eyes.

Suddenly a second face appeared in the window, the tall black-haired woman holding a sleeping Jamie.

"I'll take him back to my berth until morning. Why don't you try to get some sleep too?"

I thanked her and followed her from the dining car. *She's right,* I thought. *There's nothing else I can do tonight.*

The doctor met me at the door to the sleeper car. "Miss Spencer, I have given Mrs. McCall a sleeping powder. She shouldn't awaken until morning. And don't worry about the baby; I've taken care of everything." He patted my shoulder. "You look like you could use one of those powders too."

I shook my head. "No, I'll fall asleep easily now, thank you."

"When Mrs. McCall awakens, send for the conductor; he can explain the arrangements I've made for the body."

Absently, I nodded and made my way toward my berth. I paused when I heard the conductor call my name. "Miss Spencer, I found the baby's nurse." I turned and saw he had a sobbing Else firmly by the wrist. "She was hiding in one of the washrooms."

"Oh, yes, thank you." The agony on Else's face broke through my own cloud of grief. I rushed to her side. "Else, are you all right?"

She shook free of the conductor's grasp. "I won't go back to the old country. Don't let them send me back to Poland."

I grabbed hold of her forearms and stared into her frightened eyes. "Else, no one is going to send you back to Poland. You didn't harm the baby. Agatha was sick."

She searched my eyes. "Mrs. McCall says I killed her baby. I didn't. The baby was sleeping in her basket at the foot of my bed. After I finished nursing her, I napped."

I led Else to an empty seat. "Tell me everything that happened."

"When I woke up from my nap, I went to the necessary room. When I returned I checked on the baby." The woman paused, gulped, and inhaled deeply. "She wasn't breathing. I didn't know what to do. Mary must have heard my cry, for she suddenly grabbed the baby and began screaming at me. She said they would deport me for killing her baby." Else broke into a new round of tears.

What next? I gave her a little shake to get her attention. "No one is going to deport you, I promise. You didn't hurt Baby Agatha in any way."

Else shook her head again and again. "I can't go back to the old country. I can't go back to the old country."

A low growl from the closest sleeping compartment reminded me that people were trying to sleep. "Else, I don't know about you, but I'm exhausted. All of this can be sorted out in the morning. Why don't we both try to sleep?"

She nodded and opened the curtain to her berth. I did the same. I remember awakening once as the train stopped, to take on freight, but was soon lulled back to sleep by the familiar rocking motion of the train.

I awoke to the sound of excited voices in the corridor and pulled back the curtains. The conductor stood with his back toward me. I peered around him to see Mary, her face contorted with anger.

"Mary, what is it?" I rushed to her side. Her balled fist pounded on the edge of the mattress.

"I've been robbed! How could anyone do such a thing? I've been as generous as I possibly could with her, and she repaid me by robbing me and killing my child!"

I gaped in stunned silence as the conductor hastened to explain. "Miss Spencer, it seems that Mrs. McCall's purse and jewelry pouch are missing. Mrs. McCall seems to think that Mrs. Beck crept in and took them while she slept."

I turned to Mary. "Did you see her?"

"No, I was too drugged."

I looked from Mary to the conductor, then back again.

"Then how do you know it was she?"

Mary clicked her tongue in derision. "Who else would have known where my purse was? I know you'd never do such a thing!"

I remembered Pa's coin, and a rush of heat suffused my face and neck. "Is it possible that you placed the purse and the jewelry somewhere else and forgot?"

Mary shook her head even as I spoke. "Don't be ridiculous, Chloe. You're so young and innocent. I know it's hard for you to believe that anyone could be so dishonest."

Again I felt the heat rise in my neck and face. "Well, this should be very easy to solve. Let's just search her luggage."

The conductor scratched his head. "We would if we could, but no one can find her. Did you see her after we spoke last evening?"

I thought for a moment. "Well, no. Have you checked the necessary room?"

The conductor straightened and gazed disdainfully down the aisle. "Of course, Miss Spencer; I have also checked her berth. And it appears that all of her personal belongings are missing too."

"You won't mind if I see for myself, will you?" Stepping to the next berth, I flung the curtains back to find a perfectly made bed. Not one trace of Else remained. "This doesn't make sense. Where could she hide on a moving train? Wait, didn't we make a stop in the night?"

The conductor cleared his throat. "Er, yes, to take on freight in Springfield."

Mary gasped, "Oh, no, my mother's emerald brooch."

I whirled to face the railroad official. "Well, what are you going to do about Mrs. McCall's property?"

"The railroad will hire Pinkerton agents, of course, to pursue the matter. I will telegraph a message to the

Springfield station immediately. And, you, Mrs. McCall, if you will fill out a description form of everything that is missing?"

Mary brushed the curls off her forehead, which glistened with beads of sweat. "Will you help me with that, Chloe?"

"Of course. By the way, sir, did anyone unload Mrs. McCall's steamer trunks?"

"No, ma'am, they are still in the freight car." The conductor tipped his hat and excused himself.

As the man strode away, Mary threw herself into my arms. "Chloe, I can't take any more. I just can't take any more. First my baby, now my family heirlooms." Her tears evolved into violent coughing.

"I'm sorry, Mary." I soothed her and led her to an empty seat in the seating area. "I'm so sorry."

When her coughing subsided, she continued, "The doctor said he'd take care of everything with a funeral director when we reach Kansas City. James is meeting us there, right?"

I nodded. Her fingers knotted and unknotted the braided ties to her satin robe. "I think I'd like Agatha to be buried in our family plot in Massachusetts." She searched my eyes for approval.

Before noon, the train pulled into Kansas City, Missouri, amid a flourish of whistles and steam. Mary and I'd been packed and ready to disembark long before breakfast. The raven-haired woman had returned Jamie to me as the train slowed at the city limits. I thanked her profusely for her help. With all that had happened, I'd almost forgotten the confused little boy with the sad brown eyes still clutching the top of the red felt pouch. Despite Mary's eagerness to see James, I insisted that she remain in her berth until her husband could assist her off the train.

As we pulled into the station, I fussed with Jamie's shirt and collar while the rush of passengers disembarked. As they passed by our seat, I endured their looks of curiosity and sympathy by scanning the crowd of faces waiting on the platform. *James McCall. Where are you, James McCall?*

"Miss Spencer?" The conductor smiled down at me. "I've arranged for all your party's luggage to be unloaded. I'll send a porter to help you disembark from the train. Also Dr. Morrow has arranged for the body to be taken to the Adams's Mortuary on Second Street." Kindness surfaced in his matter-of-fact expression as he gazed at the solemn little boy in my arms.

"Thank you, thank you for everything. Mr. McCall will be here to meet us. He'll assist his wife from the train."

The crusty railroad man cleared his throat and whispered Godspeed. He patted Jamie's tightly fisted hand and hurried from the car.

With my free hand, I grabbed the satchel filled with Jamie's things and made my way up the aisle. A porter met me at the door, took the satchel from my hand, and helped me down the steps. The man escorted me over to an empty bench and set the satchel beside it. "Now you will be all right, won't you, miss?"

I smiled up at the porter. "Yes, thank you."

The porter left as a tall, gaunt man sporting a full brown mustache and a carefully tailored suit strode over and tipped his hat. An equally angular woman with fly-away hair and a scowl worthy of an Eastern schoolmarm stood at his elbow.

The stranger glanced around me instead of at me. "Miss Spencer?"

"Yes?" I extended my free hand. "You must be Mr. McCall."

He tipped his hat. "Where is my wife? Is she all right? Does she need my help from the train?"

"She's fine, though she's very weak." I nodded and pointed toward the sleeper car. "Your daughter, I don't know how to—"

Without waiting for me to finish speaking, he bounded across the platform and up the steps into the sleeper coach. I glanced from the coach, to Jamie, then at the woman.

"His son . . ."

"Mary's safety is the only thought on that boy's mind right now. The world rotates around her, as far as James is concerned." The woman shook her head and extended her arms toward Jamie.

"And this little man must be my grandnephew."

Jamie buried his head in my skirts. Gently, I disentangled him from my crinolines and urged him to give his great-aunt a hug. A tenderness came into her blue eyes as she held out her hand. Never moving a muscle, he stared up at her with his probing gaze.

She glanced at me. The start of a smile edged her cord-thin lips. "Let me introduce myself. I'm Beatrice McCall, James's aunt." A gleam of suspicion filled the woman's eyes as she scanned the russet silk traveling dress I'd chosen to wear. "Call me Aunt Bea. And I didn't catch your name."

"I'm Chloe Spencer, your niece's friend and, uh, traveling companion. We met on the train, and I agreed to accompany her to Kansas."

The woman glanced about, then asked, "Where is this Mrs. Beck and the new baby?"

I explained about the tragedy of the night before. "As for Mrs. Beck, I really can't tell you."

The woman snapped, "What do you mean, you can't tell me?"

I cleared my throat. "It's a long story."

"Well, fortunately, we have plenty of time to hear all about it on the ride home. In the meantime, James has arranged for us to stay at the Teasdale Boardinghouse here in Kansas City overnight."

On the ride to the boardinghouse, Mary and I told James and Aunt Bea about the missing wet nurse and the theft. The older woman sputtered about the loss of Mary's emerald brooch the rest of the ride. After settling us in the rooms he'd reserved for us, James left to make the necessary burial arrangements for the baby. I took a long-awaited bath in a large copper tub the maid filled for me.

That evening, James arranged to take his meal upstairs with his wife and son. Since we were the only boarders at the time, that left Aunt Bea and me to eat alone in the dining room. I'd barely sat down when the woman demanded I tell her the story again, from the beginning of Mary's labor until we arrived at Kansas City. Jamie showed up at our table during the dessert course. I took him on my lap and shared my gingersnaps with him.

When I'd answered all Aunt Bea's questions regarding our journey, she wanted to know all about me and my family. She clucked her tongue in displeasure when I told her about running away from home.

"Your poor parents. It looks like you got yourself in a worse mess. I hope you learned your lesson, young lady."

Jamie shrank from the woman's forceful voice and aggressive manner. As for me, I felt I was being broiled over live coals. While the woman held my mother's Irish heritage suspect, she did approve of my father's lineage. If she'd had her way, she would have uncovered my family heritage back to Mary, queen of Scots.

"Now that James and I are here to care for Mary and the boy, I see no reason why, when we get to Hays, you can't continue on to San Francisco."

If she imagined I'd be disturbed by her suggestion, she was wrong. I brightened. "Really? I'll talk with Mary about it in the morning.

"Jamie, why don't you go up to my room and play. I'll be along in a minute." Eagerly, he slipped off my lap and darted from the room.

Excusing myself from the table a few minutes later, I hurried upstairs. Long golden rays of light bathed the room in inviting sepia tones. Jamie sat in the middle of the braided rug, stringing brightly colored beads on a piece of yarn. Closing the bedroom door behind me, I sank onto the downy mattress, a delightful change after the rigid wooden berth on the sleeper car. I rolled over onto my stomach and watched the little boy arrange the giant wooden beads according to color and size.

A light breeze from the open window broke the stillness of the midsummer air inside the room. I thought about leaving and felt a twinge of sadness. I'd miss Mary—I'd come to care for her during the last few days. *And Jamie, ah, Jamie.*

I cupped my chin in my hands and stared out the window. All I could see were the tops of the trees beside the boardinghouse and a patch of golden sky. *By the end of the week, I could be in California.* The idea excited me. As the shadows filled the room, I prepared Jamie and myself for bed. I pulled the covers back; it was too warm for blankets. I climbed onto the bed, and Jamie curled up beside me. After emitting one ragged sigh, he fell asleep.

What is going through that tired little brain of yours? I listened to his strong, steady breathing until I, too, drifted off to sleep.

I awoke the next morning to a knock on the bedroom door. At first I was disoriented, then I remembered—Kansas City, Missouri, the Teasdale Boardinghouse. Jamie grunted and rolled over on his other side. I threw on a dressing robe, stumbled to the door, and opened it.

The shadow of James McCall filled the doorway. He handed me a lighted kerosene lamp. "Miss Spencer, our train leaves the station in two hours. Can you be ready to leave in an hour? Please send Jamie to me as soon as he's dressed."

"Yes, of course." I hastily washed and dressed Jamie, then sent him to his father. I closed the door behind him and stepped behind the dressing screen in the corner of the room to dress. As I slipped out of my rumpled nightdress, I was glad that I had bathed before dinner the evening before. I brushed my curls into a tight bun and pinned it atop my head. Carefully, I lowered the green lawn dress over my head, to the pleasant memory of my day in Chicago with Cy Chamberlain.

When I arrived at the breakfast table, it was evident that the heir apparent had jangled everybody's nerves. The father stood to one side of the heavy oak sideboard, glaring at the child. Aunt Bea, who had claimed to have everything under control, paced back and forth in front of the silk-tasseled archway, wringing her hands.

"Do something, Miss Spencer!" Aunt Bea demanded. "The child refuses to eat. I knew there was a valid reason why I never wanted children!" She huffed her way to the chair across the table from Jamie and sat down. Once seated, she helped herself to a generous stack of flapjacks, spreading a thick layer of butter on each.

"It's not my place to . . . Perhaps you, Mr. McCall, or your wife . . ."

"My wife will be down later. She's having a difficult

morning," the irate father grunted. Pain filled his eyes. "My son's terrified of me. He cringes every time I come near him!"

I hurried to Jamie and whispered into the child's ear, "Jamie, if you're not hungry, it's all right, but it's a long train ride to Hays. You're going to get mighty hungry. Try a bite of Mrs. Teasdale's flapjack." With his fork, I cut off a small piece of pancake, dipped it in a puddle of maple syrup, and held it to his mouth.

Jamie's eyes met mine. Anger and confusion battled with his desire to please me. When his stomach growled, I knew I'd won the skirmish.

His mouth opened, and I propelled the fork inside. James threw me a look of gratitude. The exasperated aunt looked up from her food.

"He knows me," I said, trying to appease his relatives. "All our normal routines are upset. Jamie has had more disruptions in two weeks of life than many of us have through adulthood."

Once his resolve was compromised, Jamie wolfed down his stack of flapjacks and drank half a glass of milk. Aunt Bea huffed and returned her attention to the shrinking mound of pancakes on her plate. James mumbled a threat about getting control of the child once he got home.

When the carriage and driver arrived to take us to the station, James helped Mary down the stairs. She wore her grief like a sealskin cape on a frigid arctic night. The easy camaraderie she and I had previously shared was gone. Aunt Bea tried to bring her out of herself, but failed. Only James could elicit a response from her.

Our carriage stopped in front of the station seconds before our train arrived. James helped Mary to the sleeper car. Aunt Bea marched toward the passenger car, expecting me to follow. No one offered to assist me with Jamie. By silent consent, he had become my charge. And the look on the older woman's face warned us to sit elsewhere. I urged the child through the first day coach into the second and found an empty seat halfway back on the left.

The comfort of the Union Pacific passenger cars did not measure up to that of the Atchison, Topeka and Sante Fe. Gone was the excitement I'd felt leaving Chicago. My heart ached for the McCall family, torn apart by their recent loss; each appeared isolated in his own pain. Within minutes the Kansas City station disappeared behind us.

Miles of endless prairie flashed by. Jamie napped on the seat beside me, his head resting in my lap. Stiff from hours of sitting on the metal-framed seat, I squirmed. Between the seat and the unevenness of the track, my patience wore thin. The unrelenting sun beat in through the dusty window, and the temperature soared.

I glanced at my fellow travelers. A cowboy slumped on the seat behind me, rhythmically twirling his hat and singing in a low voice what had to be the only tune he knew, "Oh, Suzanna."

Two veterans of the Civil War, one a Confederate and one a Union soldier, argued about the war, recounting so many battle experiences I wondered how they'd managed to survive. A plaid-suited salesman across the aisle from us kept trying to catch my eye. I think he assumed I was a widow traveling alone with my child. When the water boy passed with his copper bucket, the salesman offered me first drink—after first polishing the rim of the glass with his shirt sleeve.

I cringed inwardly at the hazards of sharing a common glass with every other passenger on the train, yet accepted it gratefully. Surely dying of a sizzling fever couldn't be much worse than the suffocating heat inside the coach. I considered waking Jamie, but when I looked at his peaceful face, I decided to let him sleep. His dreams had to be better than this oven of reality.

The water boy moved on. I stared out the window. The monotonous landscape faded out of focus, and I caught my own tired reflection staring back. Dark circles ringed my eyes. I saw with alarm that my wide green eyes looked bright with fever, and my normally pale cheeks radiated crimson blotches. Even my freckles disappeared in a blaze of color. A hairpin dangled from a kinky ringlet that had escaped the tight bun atop my head. *Could I have smallpox?*

I touched the back of my hand to each cheek. No, it was just plain hot! I squinted through the dusty window at the glaring sun and asked myself what had brought me to this parched, hot prairie. Except for the occasional sod house or rambling shed, the miles across Kansas merged into one boring experience. *So this is what it's like in Kansas—little excitement and a good deal of pain. Was it less than two weeks ago I had hid in a Pennsylvania cornfield, clutching Ma's flour sack, thrilled at the prospect of adventure?*

When the train finally slowed beside a ramshackle postmaster's shack, the cowboy behind me rose to his feet and flung his guitar over his shoulder. "Boy, it feels good to finally see the sights of home."

As he swaggered down the aisle and swung off the train while it was still moving, I searched the landscape for a glimpse of the sights he might have missed. But from where I sat, nothing had changed in the past several hours. We could have been riding in giant lazy circles, like a child's toy train under the Christmas tree, and never have known it. A hiss of steam, and the giant black monster resumed speed.

Out of the corner of my eye, I saw the salesman spit on his hand and use the moisture to pat down his greasy brown hair. He pasted a broad grin on his pocked face and leaned across the aisle. "Ma'am?" Fortunately, I guessed his intentions in time to close my eyes and feign sleep.

Droplets of sweat falling off my eyebrows stung my eyes. I wiped my forehead with my sleeve, then dabbed at my neck and chin. I'd never been so uncomfortable in my life. The swaying of the train lulled me into a dazed stupor.

Just as I was certain I could stand my discomfort no longer, James walked up the aisle and sat across from me, next to the salesman.

"Miss Spencer, we need to talk."

For a moment he picked at imaginary specks of lint on his linen trousers. He'd barely acknowledged my presence up to this point. Yet his nervousness didn't surprise me. As his pause grew in length, a knot of fear tightened in my stomach.

There had been no mention of payment since Chicago. I knew Else Beck had bolted with all of Mary's cash, but I hoped James would be able to make up the loss. Suppressing the wild thought that I'd be stuck in Kansas without money to complete my journey to California, I decided to face my fears head on.

"Mr. McCall, is there a problem? Have you arranged for my passage on to San Francisco, uninterrupted?"

"Miss Spencer, uh, I don't know quite how to ask you this." His hesitation pulled the knot in my stomach a little tighter. "Aunt Beatrice and I have been talking and, well, neither of us seem to be able to handle Jamie. Mary could, but she's too distraught over the baby's death." He paused long enough to run his fingers through his curly hair. "Such a tragedy so soon after birth! Did Mary tell you that her doctor in Boston advised her against this pregnancy in the first place? And did she tell you about her health problem?"

I frowned and shook my head slowly. His copper-brown eyes darkened to ebony. "Our family physician told her she has a spot on one lung—tuberculosis." When he saw the distress in my face, he hastened to explain. "She didn't tell me either until I'd purchased the land here in Kansas and sent for her. I threatened to sell out and return home, but she insisted that the cleaner air of the prairies would be better for her than the air pollution in a big city like Boston. I guess I wanted to believe her . . ."

"I'm sorry."

"Well, it's just something we have to deal with. That's why we need you. When we left Hays for Kansas City, Aunt Bea thought she'd have no problem caring for all three of them, Mary, the new baby, and Jamie." He chuckled, then a look of fear replaced his humor. "Don't get me wrong. Aunt Bea is a good woman, but she's never had children of her own. She was the youngest of three."

I smiled politely, for suddenly I knew what James was trying to tell me. Visions of palm trees and ocean waves vanished as he spoke.

"I know you have plans to meet your brother in San Francisco. And if Mary didn't need you desperately, I wouldn't even consider asking you this."

Beneath the hem of my skirt, I tapped out an impatient cadence with the toe of my shoe. I wanted to yell, "Just say it, will you?" Instead I swallowed the temptation and simply said, "Yes?"

"I telegraphed Mary's older sister Drucilla and asked her to come to Kansas to help with Jamie until Mary regains her strength."

"Wonderful." I hoped my relief didn't show.

"Yes, well, Dru will be a big help, no doubt." James glanced at me, reddened, then looked out the window. "The problem is, she needs time to—she's just not a very spontaneous person. In the meantime, until she can get here, Mary needs someone. And, frankly, she prefers you."

I inhaled slowly. "How long do you expect it might take before Mary's sister arrives?"

"I'm sure Drucilla will want to be here before the end of September. Besides, that would give you time to cross the Rocky Mountains and the Sierra Nevada before snow closes the passes." He lifted his head slowly and gazed pleadingly at me. I frowned and glanced out the window.

A farm horse with a young boy astride galloped on the dirt road alongside the train. When the engineer sounded the whistle, the rider waved his hat in the air. The whistle blew again. As the train slowed, I caught a glimpse of a church steeple and a collection of unpainted, drab wooden buildings.

I don't want to stay in this ugly place any longer. I don't want to put my dreams on hold any longer. Don't ask me to do this, Lord. After all, Joe is waiting for me in California—and so is Cy.

The Letter Home

"Mr. McCall, I will agree to postpone my trip long enough to get Jamie settled, but no longer. After that, you might want to hire one of the local women until Mary's sister arrives." I'd never been able to quit once I'd started something. Pa considered it a positive trait. Now I wasn't so sure.

Mr. McCall frowned and pursed his lips. "All right, we'll gladly take whatever you can give."

"One more thing," I added. "I would feel more secure if you would purchase my ticket for San Francisco today while we're in town."

The man's face hardened. He stood up to his full six feet, three inches. "I can assure you, Miss Spencer, you will be reimbursed for your assistance. When a McCall gives his word, he always keeps it."

I blushed. "Please don't take offense. I just meant—"

"I know what you meant, Miss Spencer!" He tugged at his vest. "If you will excuse me, I must help my wife. I would appreciate it if you would continue to care for my son; thank you."

I tried to think of something to say. *Don't say anything, stupid. You've said enough.* James McCall strode stiffly out of the day coach.

Moments later, the train eased to a stop in Hays. I

awakened Jamie and gathered up our belongings.

The raw vitality of Hays accosted me the moment my feet touched the depot's wooden platform. I'd expected a lazy little hamlet like some I'd seen from the train window. Instead, I stared in fascination at the sprawling, boisterous town that had grown up beside Fort Hays.

James led us to a wooden bench beside the depot. Mary immediately sat down and leaned her head back against the building. As I stood beside the bench, I whispered to Aunt Bea, "There are so many people. The town has the vigor of Chicago. Where do they all come from?"

She laughed aloud for the first time. "Eastern dudes, cowboys from outlying cattle ranches, farmers and their wives shopping for winter, land speculators, gamblers, fancy ladies, fortune seekers, and misfits—you name it, and Hays has it." She lifted her chin in pride. This was her town, and she loved it. "Used to have upwards of one thousand residents, but the nineties haven't been good to people in these parts. Things are looking up, though, what with the rumors that the U.S. government plans to grant Fort Hays to the state as a normal school to train teachers." She waved at the baggage boy standing next to the locomotive. "I run the feed and hardware store at the edge of the city."

"Really? A feed and hardware store?" I couldn't believe the change in this woman once she was back on familiar soil. She even talked differently.

"The feed and hardware store for these parts. Guess it is a mighty unusual occupation for a woman." She grinned. "I was twenty-two when Chester, my husband, died in a flash flood over at Big Creek. My family in Boston tried to convince me to sell out and head east, but I stayed on. That was twenty-six years ago last spring."

"I imagine it's been no easy task. You must have been tempted at times to take their advice."

"You must be joshing! What kind of life would I have, the cosseted widowed aunt? I would be consigned to raising everyone else's young-uns." The woman huffed. "Besides, the prairie has a way of growing on a body."

The arrival of a middle-aged man as black and rangy as a fire poker interrupted our conversation. The moment Aunt Beatrice spotted him making his way down the platform, she jumped to her feet and rushed to him. He tipped his worn wide-brimmed hat respectfully to each of us.

"Where have you been, Sam? James has been looking for you," the woman demanded.

"He found me, ma'am, and sent me to fetch you ladies." The man directed his attention toward Mary. She opened her eyes. "You must be James's Mary. He said to tell you that he had business to tend to and he'd meet us at the carriage."

Realizing I'd been staring, I reddened and looked away. A tug on my sleeve, and Aunt Beatrice's hearty voice broke through my thoughts. "Sam, I want you to meet Miss Spencer. She'll be staying with James and Mary for a short time. Chloe, Sam is James's foreman."

"It's an honor, miss." The man tipped his hat and extended his hand toward the satchel I was carrying. Involuntarily, I drew back from contact. When I realized what I'd done, I tried to apologize. A wide grin filled his face. "That's all right, Miss Spencer. It won't rub off, you know."

He'd read my mind. My face flared fiery red. Flustered, I cast about for an appropriate response, but none came. Mary saved me by requesting that he help her to the carriage and come back later for the luggage.

"Mr. James has arranged to have the luggage delivered." The hired man took Mary's arm. Aunt Beatrice, Jamie, and I followed behind, with the three smaller satchels. Sam helped Mary then Aunt Beatrice into the carriage. When he extended his hand toward me, I felt I had to say something. "I meant no offense. Honest."

"Now, don't you worry a bit, miss. No offense was taken." He lifted Jamie into the front seat with him, then climbed aboard to await James's return.

Next to me, Mary and her aunt were discussing the night's sleeping arrangements, or I should say, Aunt Beatrice was imposing her plans, and Mary was protesting. "I really do think it would be best, and goodness knows, I have enough room. You look too peaked to travel any farther today. I am sure James will agree." Aunt Beatrice perked up the drooping sleeves of her muslin traveling dress.

"But I do so want to see the home he bought for me," Mary's voice drifted off in defeat. She sighed and leaned back against the carriage's leather seat.

James emerged from the depot, strode across the carriage lot, and leaped aboard the waiting buggy next to his son. Sam flicked the reins and urged the team of horses forward.

The carriage bounced over the unpaved, rutted streets. I clung to the edge of the seat until my knuckles turned white. The vehicle swayed precariously as Sam maneuvered around deep ruts and at the same time tried to avoid hitting a drunk who staggered into our path.

In a round, definite tone, James announced, "Mary, Aunt Bea and I have agreed that it would be wise for you to rest up at her place for a day or two before traveling to our ranch. Of course, I'll need to go on ahead. I'll come back for you after you've rested up a bit."

Mary nodded reluctantly. Feeling her disappointment, I directed my attention to the businesses lining the street: Dalton's Saloon, M. E. Joyce—justice of the peace, Mrs. Gowdy's Dress Shop, Mose Walter's Saloon, the Perty Hotel, White's Barber Shop, and Paddy Welch's Saloon and Gambling House. I'd never seen so many saloons in my life. We drove past Hamlin's General Store, the Hays Free Press, and Treat's Candy and Peanut Stand. Some of the businesses stood idle; others thrived.

Aunt Beatrice interrupted my thoughts. "We had a fire in 1895, the worst fire in the town's history. Eighty-seven buildings were destroyed. It was a terrible blow to the town."

The business district stopped abruptly at one corner, and the residential section began—a variety of unpainted, clapboard houses in a row. A mangy-looking dog ran out from behind Maybelle's Boardinghouse. He barked at the horses' heels, causing them to shy, but Sam handled the team skillfully.

As the carriage came to a stop in front of the McCall Feed and Hardware Store, I heaved a sigh of relief. The two-story, boxlike building sported a fading coat of whitewash.

"I live up top." Aunt Beatrice pointed to the windows on the second floor. She climbed out of the carriage and strode inside the store before Sam could assist her.

We were met at the door by a big-boned, smiling woman. It was difficult to tell where her sun-tanned complexion ended and her brown hair began. Aunt Beatrice introduced her as Zerelda Paget.

"Zerelda insisted on being here when you arrived, Mary. She's your next-door neighbor out at the ranch. She has twin boys of her own."

Zerelda's brown eyes lighted up at the sight of Jamie.

She scooped him into her arms with the ease of a veteran. "You poor thing. You must be stifling in all those clothes. Why don't you come with me, and we'll find Billy and Benny."

Zerelda took the satchel from my hand and disappeared with Jamie through a door in the back of the store.

Out of the corner of my eye, I noticed Aunt Beatrice bristle. I turned my face away from her to hide my smile. Regaining her composure, Aunt Beatrice instructed me to follow her. I allowed myself to be drawn along by the raw force of her determination. Amid a steady stream of information, Aunt Beatrice led me past bins of nails, bolts, and reams of barbed wire into a large storeroom filled with wooden crates and machinery parts.

I followed my hostess up an enclosed staircase, down a hallway, and into a small bedroom under the eaves. "I put Mary and James in the guest room down the hall. I'm in the next room. I'll put the boy in the room across from you."

I glanced around at the neat, simply furnished room. White priscilla curtains fluttered in the warm breeze blowing off the prairie. A porcelain wash basin with matching pitcher sat on a washstand beneath the window. A fold-down oak desk, a matching straight chair, and a bentwood rocker sat nearby. A blue-and-white wedding ring quilt covered the giant brass bed. The woman straightened the quilt. "I hope this will be adequate."

"More than adequate. Thank you, Mrs. McCall."

"I'm afraid we got off to a bad start in Kansas City. I admit I suspected you of being a gold digger, preying on my niece—especially after I heard about the theft." She smiled at me. "I don't like admitting I'm wrong, but do you think we could start over, Miss Spencer?"

I beamed. "That would be nice. And please call me Chloe. I'm not used to such formality."

She grasped my hands in hers. "Welcome, Chloe, to Hays, Kansas, the hub of western Kansas."

The woman looked into my eyes, her forehead creased with worry. "Why doesn't the boy speak? Is he mentally deficient?"

I laughed. "His mind is faster than a steel trap, as my Pa would say. As to why he doesn't speak, I don't know if there's a physical cause or if something traumatic happened to him."

"Was he like this before Mary left Boston?"

I shook my head. "I don't know. Mary never said. She pays him little mind, I'm afraid, especially since she lost the baby."

"Well, I appreciate everything you are doing for my family, Chloe. Let me know if I can do anything in return, anything!"

"Thank you." I yawned involuntarily.

Addressing me as if she were the teacher and I were a six-year-old on the first day of school, she took me by the shoulders and directed me to the side of the bed. "You catch a nap. Zerelda will watch over Jamie until suppertime; then Sam will take her and the boys home. There's fresh water in the pitcher on the stand, and the chamber pot is in the base of the washstand."

Somehow I didn't mind being mothered once again. I bounced a little on the edge of the bed, then ran my hand over the blue rings on the quilt. "Thank you, Mrs., er, Aunt Bea, for everything. A nap sounds fabulous."

"Help yourself to the writing paper, ink, and envelopes in the desk. In fact, I am willing to pay the postage if you will write a letter home to your parents. They must be worried sick about you!"

"I can't let you do that."

"I insist!" She smiled to soften her brisk tone, turned abruptly, and left. I rolled onto my back in the middle of the bed and flung my arms out. To sleep in a real bed once more! Such luxury! I allowed the downy mattress to engulf me. The mattress at the boardinghouse had been filled with cornhusks—a fact that all the layers of bedding in the world couldn't hide.

My conscience tussled with my weariness over the letter my hostess had urged me to write. Responsibility won out. I dragged myself off the bed and made my way to the desk. I sat down and lowered the writing surface; the supplies were all there, as promised. However, after three attempts on Aunt Bea's linen stationery, I realized that writing this letter would be much more difficult than I first imagined. Scrapping my fourth start, I tried again.

"Dearest Ma and Pa, As you can tell by the postmark, I am in Hays, Kansas. It looks like I'll be staying here long enough for you to write back." I told them about Mary, the baby, about Jamie, his father, his aunt. "So, you see, I couldn't walk away from the child." I told them about Mrs. Schnetzler and the impact the woman had made on me. "She gave me many things to think about. Most of all, she helped me see that God cares for me, that I don't need to run away from my problems."

"Running away was childish. And stealing the coin was wrong. I am so sorry for that. I've asked God to forgive me. Can you? Will you? My mistakes haunt me. I need to know that you still love me and have forgiven me. When I feel comfortable enough to leave Jamie to another's care, I'll probably go on to California. (I'd never get this close again if I came home.) Kiss the boys for me. Also kiss Ori and Dorothy. Tell them I miss them, and tell Hattie I'll write soon. I love you all. Your daughter, Chloe Mae."

I blew on the paper to dry the ink, folded the letter, and addressed the envelope. A heavy weight slipped from my shoulders as I slipped the letter and the coin into the envelope. As I sealed the envelope, the guilt that had hobbled me fell away. I was free. I tossed my dress and crinolines onto the rocking chair and bounced on the bed. With my mind released from the past, I eagerly anticipated the future.

Thank You, Father. I rolled over onto my back and shut my eyes. *I don't know where You and I are heading, but I know it's going to be a terrific journey.*